SWEEP #9

Strife

Cate Tiernan

PUFFIN BOOKS

All quoted materials in this work were created by the author.
Any resemblance to existing works is accidental.

Strife

Puffin Books
Published by the Penguin Group
Penguin Putnam Books for Young Readers,
345 Hudson Street, New York, New York 10014, U.S.A.
Penguin Books Ltd, 80 Strand, London WC2R 0RL, England
Penguin Books Australia Ltd, Ringwood, Victoria, Australia
Penguin Books Canada Ltd, 10 Alcorn Avenue, Toronto, Ontario, Canada M4V 3B2
Penguin Books (N.Z.) Ltd, 182-190 Wairau Road, Auckland 10, New Zealand

Penguin Books Ltd, Registered Offices: Harmondsworth, Middlesex, England

Published by Puffin Books,
a division of Penguin Putnam Books for Young Readers, 2001

1 3 5 7 9 10 8 6 4 2

Cover Photography (foreground) copyright Wayne Eastep/Getty Images/Stone
Cover Photography (background) by Trinette Read/nonstøck
Photo-illustration by Marci Senders
Series design by Russell Gordon

Produced by 17th Street Productions,
an Alloy Online, Inc. company
151 West 26th Street
New York, NY 10001

17th Street Productions and associated logos
are trademarks and/or registered trademarks of Alloy, Inc.

ISBN 0-14-230107-8

Printed in the United States of America

To the real Erin Murphy

1.
The Meeting

August 28, 1971

At the end of the summer the sea always seems to be railing against the thought of another long, fierce New England winter. The waves hurtle themselves against the rocks with blind rage. Fishermen think of August as a terrifying month, but for me, it's the most thrilling. Maybe it's because my family has lived in Gloucester for generations. Or maybe it's because we're Wiccans, and that puts us in greater tune with nature.

It's ironic to think that my family settled so close to Salem—we were very lucky to survive the witch trials. It's strange to think that Wicca could inspire such terror when it's such a gentle, loving, nurturing religion. I guess people are always afraid of power that they don't understand. And Wicca does deal with raw power, although the way my family practices it, it's never *destructive. Both Mom and Dad are very into responsible uses of magick, which they drummed into me before my initiation three years ago. Now they are teaching the same thing to my younger brother, Sam. He won't be initiated for another seven months, but already I can see the energy beginning to spark in him. I know he's going to be a powerful witch. I'm looking forward to his rites, but it's hard not to envy him sometimes. My own power is more fickle, although I like to think that it is growing as I continue to study and practice.*

Every day I pray to the Goddess to make me worthy of my family.

—Sarah Curtis

Calm down, I told myself as I gazed into the bathroom mirror and struggled to pull my long brown hair into a tidy French braid. This is going to be fine. I glanced at my watch. My boyfriend, Hunter Niall, was due any minute. Normally I would have been thrilled to be spending an evening with him, but tonight was no ordinary night. No—tonight was the official meet-the-parents dinner, and I was beginning to feel sick with tension.

I was distracted by a quick tap on the door.

"Come in," I called.

My sister, Mary K., walked into the bathroom. "Is that what you're wearing?" she asked, staring at my faded blue jeans and soft purple fleece shirt.

I looked down at my outfit. "What's wrong with this?"

Mary K. just sighed and marched through the bathroom to the door that led into my bedroom.

"Where are you going?" I asked.

"To find that shirt Aunt Eileen gave you for Christmas," Mary K. said. "I know it'll look great on you, and besides, she and Paula are already downstairs, waiting for us."

"That shirt is practically see-through!" I argued as Mary K. rummaged through my drawers.

"Which is why you'll wear it with this," she countered, holding up a pale pink tank top. Mary K. pulled the sheer, stretchy shirt off a hanger in my closet and handed it and the tank top to me. "At least you're wearing superlow jeans," she said as I yanked off my fleece. "You've got the body for them."

I pulled on the new outfit and stared at myself in the bathroom mirror. The slate blue shirt did make my dark eyes seem warmer, and the pink tone of the tank made my skin rosy. Once again, I was amazed at my sister's ability to pull together an outfit based on clothes I hardly ever wore.

Just then the doorbell rang. "Show time!" Mary K. said brightly.

I stifled a groan. For the hundredth time, I wanted to kick myself for letting my parents invite Hunter over for dinner. It had seemed like a good idea when Mom suggested it, but now that the night had arrived, my heart was racing. It didn't help that my mom had decided to make a big event out of it, pulling together an ambitious dinner menu and inviting my aunt Eileen and her girlfriend, Paula, over, too. What if they don't like him? I worried as I stared at my reflection. My parents had met Hunter before but only briefly, in casual settings. Comparatively, this felt more like a college entrance exam.

I could hear the muted sound of greetings in the front hall. Mary K. pulled on her sweater. "Let's go," she said.

I followed her into the hall and down the stairs. Hunter was in the front alcove, shaking hands with my father and smiling at my aunt and her girlfriend. He was holding a paper cone of roses—they were such a delicate pink that they seemed to glow with their own light, like a bouquet of pearls. I stopped on the steps, and Hunter looked up at me with his steady green gaze. I smiled, and he smiled back, the edges of his brilliant eyes crinkling in a way that was both exciting and familiar.

"Hey, Morgan," my aunt Eileen said with a grin. "That shirt looks great on you." Her back was to Hunter, and she waggled her eyebrows at me, as if to say, "He's cute." I laughed nervously and gave her and Paula a hello hug.

Hunter gave me a quick kiss on the cheek. "You look beautiful," he whispered, and I felt a blush rise to my face.

Mary K. took a delicate sniff. "Is something on fire?" she asked.

My dad looked at me in alarm, his eyes huge behind his glasses.

"I think I'd better go see how Mom is doing," I said quickly. "Shall I put these in some water?" I asked Hunter, taking the roses from him. "They're gorgeous."

"Do you need help?" Hunter asked.

"Oh, no," I said as nonchalantly as I could. "I'm sure everything is under control."

Hunter smiled, and I knew he wasn't fooled for a second.

My dad led everyone into the living room as I hurried into the kitchen. My mom was frantically waving her arms in a desperate attempt to force the smoke pouring from the oven out the open back door.

"Should I do something?" I asked.

"Oh, Morgan!" Relief swept over my mom's face. "Would you put on the fan before the fire alarm goes off? I have to pull this roast out of the oven—I think some of the drippings caught on fire." My mother is a real estate broker and doesn't spend a lot of time in the kitchen. The fact that my parents had both volunteered to cook for Hunter—Dad made his famous black-bottom pie for dessert—was just evidence of how special they wanted this night to be.

I put the roses on the countertop, flipped on the fan, and turned the flame under the carrots on the stove to low as my mom wrestled the roast from the oven and fanned the smoke away from it. She shook her head. "We should have ordered out," she said mournfully, pondering the blackened mess.

I tried not to groan out loud. "Maybe we can make some gravy to cover up the black parts," I suggested.

Mom nodded, straightening her red sweater while I pulled some instant gravy out of the cabinet. "Thank you," she said, giving me a wry smile. "I guess I'd better get out there and say hello to Hunter."

Something in my mother's voice made me look at her. Until that moment, it hadn't occurred to me that my mom might be as nervous about tonight's official meet and greet as I was.

My mom picked up the cone of roses. "These are beautiful," she said. After a moment she added, "Hunter really is nice, isn't he?"

"He really is," I agreed. My mother smiled, and I had the sudden urge to hug her. She and my father knew that Hunter was into Wicca (although they didn't know quite how deeply).

For lots of reasons, they were incredibly uncomfortable with the thought that Wicca was a part of my life. But here they were, making an extra effort to get to know Hunter, to be open-minded.

My mom hurried out to say hello to everyone. I made the gravy as Mary K. and my dad came into the kitchen. Dad did his best to carve up the roast. He really had to put his shoulder into it, but eventually he cut it into slices thin enough to be served. I put it on plates and poured gravy over each serving, then added the side dishes, and Mary K. carried the plates to the table. The roast didn't look too terrifying once it was disguised.

By the time I walked into the dining room, everyone was laughing and chatting. Hunter sent me a look that instantly made me feel warm all over, and I headed for my seat between him and Mary K.

"Now that everyone's here," Aunt Eileen said as I slid into the chair across from her, "Paula and I have some news."

"What is it?" I asked.

"We've filed our papers," Paula said with a sheepish grin.

"The adoption agency said that we should get a green light within the next ten weeks," Aunt Eileen added.

"Then you'll get a baby?" Mary K. asked. "That's great!"

I smiled, unsure what to say. I was happy for Paula and Aunt Eileen, but I couldn't help feeling a little weird. After all, I had only found out a few months before that *I* was adopted. It was a discovery that had led me to realize I was a blood witch, descended from a long line of powerful Wiccan women.

There was a moment of awkward silence, as if everyone was waiting for my response. I looked at my aunt, knowing how much she wanted me to be happy for her. "Congratulations," I said finally. "That's—that's great."

"That will be a lucky baby," Hunter said, and Aunt Eileen beamed at him.

Under the table, he reached for my hand and gave it a gentle squeeze.

Turning to my mother, Hunter held up a forkful of roast beef and said, "Mrs. Rowlands, this American smokehouse flavor is unbelievable—it's something we never get in England."

My mother hid her grin behind her napkin. "Thank you," she said.

I concentrated on my food so that I wouldn't look at him and laugh. It was strange to see Hunter acting so confident and natural with my parents. When we were alone together, he tended to be more reserved, even a little intense.

"Mr. Rowlands, Morgan tells me that you're very interested in physics," Hunter went on. "Did you happen to read that article in *Scientific American* about the neutrino collector they're building in Switzerland?"

I could see by Dad's face that this topic of conversation was his idea of heaven. Mom raised her eyebrows at me. On the other side of Hunter, Mary K. leaned back in her chair to give me a broad wink.

I couldn't believe this night was going so well.

Once we were finished with dinner, Mary K. and I cleared the table and brought out dessert plates. Then I went back into the kitchen to grab the black-bottom pie. Just as I walked in from the dining room, the back door blew open with a bang. I jumped and turned around. Was someone out there? I walked to the door and cast out my senses.

I felt nothing. I took a quick lungful of the crisp night air. It was the middle of February, and in the moonlight the trees loomed black beneath their shrouds of snow. I shivered suddenly. It's just the wind, I told myself as I crossed to the door and grabbed the doorknob. Looking out into the night, I was hit with a sudden image of my old boyfriend, Cal Blaire. His dark, shaggy hair and golden eyes swam in my brain for a dizzying second, and then, just as quickly, the image was gone, leaving me with a dull ache in my chest.

Cal.

For a moment I tried to picture this evening with Cal at the dinner table instead of Hunter, but I couldn't. Cal had introduced me to Wicca, and he had told me that he loved me and that I was special . . . but I had always felt insecure around him. Not that I'm particularly secure to begin with when it comes to guys, but there was something about Cal that made me feel like he was doing me a favor by listening to me.

It had turned out that he only got to know me in the first place because his mother, Selene, wanted to drain me of my magick. She had almost succeeded, but at the end Cal had given his life to stop her. That had left me with a deep well of confusion and sadness. Cal had betrayed me, but in his own way, he had loved me.

"Where's that pie? The natives are getting restless," Mary K. said as she strode into the kitchen. She stopped when she saw my face. "Are you okay?"

I gave my head a quick shake to clear it and shut the outside door. "Sorry." I crossed the kitchen and yanked open the fridge. "I was just off in my own world for a minute. The pie's right here." I handed it to her.

"I think this is going really well, don't you?" Mary K. asked in a low voice as she pulled open the silverware drawer and got out a knife.

"Shockingly well," I agreed. I was grateful that Mary K. was being so supportive. She wasn't exactly a huge fan of Wicca, either, but she really liked Hunter.

My dad's black-bottom pie was a treat, thick with nuts and silky chocolate. Once it was served, conversation slowed as everyone savored each bite.

"I'm stuffed," Aunt Eileen said, once she had finished her pie.

"Everything was delicious," Paula chimed in.

My dad looked around the table. "Coffee in the living room?"

"Hunter?" my mom prompted. "Coffee? Or maybe you'd like some tea?"

"Nothing for me, thanks. I'll help Morgan and Mary K. with the dishes," Hunter said. He started gathering plates. I joined in, torn between awe and embarrassment.

"How am I doing?" Hunter whispered as we walked into the kitchen.

I snorted. "I never knew you were such a ham. Or rather, such a smokehouse-flavored roast beef. I think my parents are just about ready to adopt you."

"Fine with me. Can I share your room?" He gave me a look, and my heartbeat suddenly picked up.

"Eww, Morgan!" Mary K. said from the sink, where she was scraping food into the garbage disposal. "Is this your plate? I can't believe you hid your roast beef under a pile of mashed potatoes!"

"Well, you didn't expect me to eat it, did you?" I countered. "I didn't see you asking for seconds, either."

"I don't like red meat," Mary K. said primly.

"I thought the roast beef was good," Hunter said, looking surprised.

Mary K. and I snickered. "Well, he is British," Mary K. pointed out.

"I thought you were just sucking up to my mom," I told Hunter. "The fact that you were actually sincere is a little scary. Should I worry about you?"

Hunter laughed, and I felt a rush of delight. It was a surprising sound—deep and rich—and one I didn't hear all that often, especially lately. A few weeks ago Hunter and I had gone to New York to investigate Amyranth, a coven of Woodbane witches. The Woodbanes were one of the Seven Great Clans of Wicca—the ancient clans of blood witches. Historically, Woodbanes were dedicated to expanding their own power at any cost.

In a horrible surprise we'd discovered that one of Amyranth's leaders, and the man who killed my birth mother, was actually my birth father, Ciaran MacEwan. Ciaran had almost killed me, too, before he realized I was his daughter. The realization that I had come from someone so totally evil had thrown me into a tailspin, and for a while Hunter and I had broken up. During that time, Ciaran had manipulated me into almost killing him. But now we were back together—ironically, thanks to Ciaran—and Hunter's warm laugh in my family's bright yellow kitchen made all the horrible things we'd been through seem like they'd happened ages ago instead of only weeks.

"All right, Mary K.," I said, "I'll scrape the dishes if you'll clear off the table."

"Deal," she said, wiping her hands on a towel.

"You scrape, I'll stack," Hunter said. Once Mary K. was out of earshot, he gestured after her. "How is she?"

I felt a pang. Twice in the last week Mary K. had woken up screaming from a nightmare about being trapped in a small room. I was worried that these dreams were tied to the night months ago when Selene had kidnapped Mary K. and used her as bait to lure me to her house. Mary K., spelled by Selene, had seemed unaware of the horrible battle Hunter and I had fought with Selene, but I always suspected that at least some part of that evening had penetrated her subconscious. Now I was afraid the suppressed knowledge might be boiling up into her conscious mind.

"She slept fine last night, as far as I know," I told Hunter.

"Morgan, I think you should tell Mary K. the truth."

"I know." I shifted uncomfortably. "You said that yesterday."

Hunter's voice was low but insistent. "She deserves to know what happened that night—partly for her own sanity."

"What happened what night?"

I wheeled and saw Mary K. standing in the doorway. "What night?" she repeated, her eyes huge. "What were you talking about? What haven't you told me?"

Her voice seemed to expand and fill the room, like thick smoke, then slowly fade away, seeping into the walls. I felt the color drain from my face.

"I—we just meant—" I stammered, turning to Hunter for help.

But Mary K. didn't even look at him. She kept her eyes trained on me. "What haven't you told me, Morgan?" she asked again. "It's about the night I was with Cal's mother, the night they both died. Isn't it?"

I didn't answer. The silence hung in the brightly lit kitchen.

Mary K.'s nostrils flared. "You told me that we were never in any danger."

I bit my lip, hesitating. *Tell her,* I could almost hear Hunter saying. A quick glance at him and I realized that he was throwing up a blocking spell so that my parents wouldn't be able to hear the argument we both knew was coming.

I sighed. "We *were* in danger," I admitted finally. "You remember that you were at Selene's house?" I could hear the waver in my own voice.

My sister nodded. A small crease formed between her eyebrows as she struggled with the memory. In addition to Selene's spell, I had thrown up a number of obscuring and look-away spells as Selene attacked me and Hunter with every weapon in her dark arsenal. Mary K., I knew, had seen very little that night and understood even less.

"Selene wanted . . . ," I started, but I couldn't force myself to say, "to steal my magick." My family was ignorant of my powers as a witch, and that was the way I wanted to keep it. I decided to start over. "Selene wanted something from me. She wanted it pretty badly, and she threatened me—and you—to get it. She would have carried out her threats, but Hunter and I managed to stop her."

"And . . ." Mary K. swallowed hard. "That's how she—died?"

"Yes." The word was a whisper.

"You *killed* her?" Mary K.'s voice was shrill.

"She was going to kill us." The words flew out of my

mouth before I could halt them. "I stopped her."

My sister's face went pale. I couldn't tell whether it was from fear or rage. "Oh my God, Morgan!" she cried. "When the hell were you going to tell me?"

"I don't know," I admitted. "But we're all okay—"

"No, we are not okay!" Mary K. burst out. "We almost died, and you *lied* to me, Morgan! You hid this from me! And you would have gone on doing it!"

"I never lied to you." The words sounded lame even to me.

"No, you just never told me the truth." Her eyes flashed.

"Mary K.—" I reached out to grab her shoulder, but she jerked away from me.

"Don't touch me," she snarled. The words hit me like a slap, and before I could gather my thoughts to respond, my sister had turned and run out of the kitchen. I stared dumbly after her, hearing her feet thud up the stairs.

"Morgan," said a soft voice behind me. Hunter.

I turned to face him, feeling beaten. "I think I'd better go," he said. His face was grim.

I sighed. "I'm sorry."

"Don't be." Hunter reached out and touched the side of my face softly. "I understand. Walk me to the door?"

I nodded. As we walked toward the living room, a burst of laughter floated into the hall. Everyone looked up as we stepped into the room.

"Hunter has to go," I announced.

"Dinner was wonderful," Hunter said warmly. "Thanks so much for having me."

"Anytime," my father said heartily. He shook Hunter's hand and grinned at him.

"It was truly our pleasure," my mom agreed as she gave Hunter a kiss on the cheek. I was blown away. My mom—who never let me or my sister have guys in our rooms—was giving Hunter the seal of approval.

"Great meeting you," Aunt Eileen said. She and Paula gave Hunter a friendly wave from the couch.

We turned and walked into the front hall. "Morgan— don't forget that you've got homework to finish," my mother called after me.

"Don't worry, I won't," I promised, grabbing my jacket from a peg in the hallway. As if I could forget. I had a ton of work to do. With all of the stuff that had been going on lately, I had fallen horrendously behind. If I didn't hand in my extra-credit paper for English the next day, I could practically kiss a passing grade good-bye.

"Listen, Morgan, there's something I have to tell you," Hunter said as we walked out onto the front stoop. His voice turned serious, and he reached behind me to pull the front door closed. "I heard from Eoife just before I came here tonight."

The cold February wind whipped against my face. "Isn't she in London?"

Hunter nodded. "She phoned. She had a message for you."

Eoife McNabb worked for the International Council of Witches, the same group Hunter worked for. She was the one who had recently asked me to help the organization by contacting my birth father. The council had been seeking Ciaran for a long time, believing that he and his coven, Amyranth, were behind the dark wave, a hideous magickal cloud of destruction that had wiped out countless covens over the years. I'd almost succeeded in trapping Ciaran, but at the last moment he'd managed to slip through all our fingers.

"Have they found Ciaran yet?" I asked.

Hunter shook his head. "Not yet, but the council is working on it. They believe he's somewhere in northern Spain or southern France. Eoife wanted you to know that the watch sigil you placed on him has been enormously helpful."

Hearing this, I felt a rush of contradictory emotions. Ciaran was my birth father, and I'd felt a strange sense of connection to him when we were together. Still, I knew he was a dangerous man, that the council needed to find him . . . and stop him.

"I just wish you had more formal training," Hunter went on. "Especially with Ciaran still at large—"

"I know," I snapped. "I'm a loose cannon. A witch with power as strong as mine has a duty. I need to see the bigger picture. Et cetera. I've heard it all before."

"I don't want anything to happen to you," Hunter whispered.

The cold around me seemed to melt away as he leaned toward me and his lips met mine.

The kiss went on and on, and for a moment I felt a strange sort of nostalgia, knowing that I couldn't be in this moment forever. Soon I would have to go back to the real world—the world in which I had homework to do and Mary K. was rightfully angry with me. But I pushed that feeling away. Don't think about what will happen when this kiss is over, I told myself.

My heart raced, and I was suddenly aware of the blood coursing through my body. I was aware of every breath of cold air that I drew into my lungs and released into the wintry night in a puff of steam. I could feel the heat that our two bodies were generating at the heart of the frigid darkness. I felt like more than just a person, and the emotions I felt seemed wilder than desire, deeper than love. I felt like I was a force of nature—a storm, something unstoppable. I felt connected to Hunter and the world around me in an intricate and inseparable way, and I knew I was part of something greater than myself.

2.
Contact

I feel sick. This afternoon Sam showed me a book he had just "discovered." When I saw the cover, I nearly dropped the book in terror. It was a first edition of Harris Stoughton's book, <u>On the Containement of Magick</u>.

I couldn't figure out where he'd found it. My parents haven't told him about their library yet, and even if they had, I doubt they own any books by Harris Stoughton. Sam told me that he'd found the book in the public library and had just taken it. He <u>stole</u> the book. He told me that he thought the book wanted him to have it.

I couldn't believe this was the brother I'd known for his entire life. I asked Sam if he had any idea who Harris Stoughton was, and of course he didn't. I should hope not. I explained that Stoughton was *the most notorious witch in New England—that he used dark magic and antiwitch hysteria to wipe out as many non-Woodbane witches as he could. He even killed a couple of our blood relatives, although I didn't tell Sam that. I could tell he felt guilty enough as it was.*

I thought that would be the end of it, but when I handed him the book and asked him what he planned to do with it, Sam just said that he wasn't sure. I know my brother. If I try to force him to get rid of it, he'll only want to hold on to it more. Part of me wants to tell our parents about this, but a larger part of me is afraid of how they'll react.

Goddess, grant me wisdom. And grant me courage to live in the house with that evil book.

—Sarah Curtis

The tall redbrick form of Widow's Vale High School rose bleakly against the gray February sky. I tried to shrug off the feeling of gloom that crept over me as I trudged toward the front door. Morning was never my finest hour, and the short winter days didn't help much. Neither did the fact that Mary K. had gotten a ride to school with her friend Susan Wallace instead of with me. She wasn't speaking to me.

"Hey, Morgan!" Jenna Ruiz stopped me as I stepped into the front hall. Her blond hair was swept up into a ponytail, and she was wearing a brown sweater and dark jeans. Her tentative smile made her look young and unsure. It was funny to remember that before I had joined the coven, I had found Jenna slightly intimidating. "Going my way?" she asked, jerking her head toward the stairwell that led down to the basement—our coven's winter hangout.

I tucked a few strands of hair behind one ear. "Where else?" I replied, and we fell into step together.

Jenna pushed open the door to the stairwell. Most of our regular coven crowd had already gathered. My good friend Robbie Gurevitch was sitting on the bottom step, leaning against Bree Warren's knees. Her arms were draped over his shoulders. Ethan Sharp and Sharon Goodfine sat higher up and to the left.

Raven Meltzer stood at the bottom of the stairs, by the banister. She was wearing a red velvet shirt and low-slung black leather pants that showed off the flame tattoo around her navel. It was actually a demure look for Raven. I, on the other hand, could never pull off that look in my wildest dreams. As I studied her, I wondered if Raven had gotten my cosmic share of curves.

The pale winter light that leaked in through the window at the top of the landing cast a faint glow on everyone's faces. I leaned against the wall by the bottom stair and Bree smiled at me, taking away at least part of the February chill.

"Hey," she said warmly. "How did it go last night?"

"Great," I replied. "Everyone was charming, everyone was charmed."

Sharon took off her baby blue cardigan and slung it over her shoulders. "What are we talking about?" she asked.

"Hunter did the official parental dinner last night," Robbie explained.

"Oh, man," Ethan said. "Cruel and unusual." Sharon dug her elbow into his knee. "Ouch!" he yelped. "I was just saying . . ."

"No, it's true," I agreed. "It was a little tense at first. But everyone was on their best behavior. It went well."

"Not surprising," Robbie said. "Hunter is every parent's dream."

I looked at him, surprised. "How so?" I asked.

Robbie shrugged. "Hunter's responsible, he's generous, he's intelligent. And everyone can see that he's good for you, Morgan."

"Besides, he's a witch," Raven added dryly. "What parent wouldn't be thrilled?"

I ignored Raven's comment, pleased with what Robbie had said. He and I were close friends, but we'd had a fight a while back. He'd thought I was misusing my powers, and he'd had a point. But I was learning to be more responsible. It was good to know that Robbie realized my relationship with Hunter was a big part of that.

"Hey, Morgan," Ethan piped up, "have you heard anything from Killian?"

Killian was Ciaran's son and my half brother. I had gotten to know him slightly over the past few weeks, but after he'd come up to visit me in Widow's Vale and behaved really badly, he'd pretty much dropped out of sight.

"No," I said, feeling a twinge of regret. Killian was irresponsible, reckless, possibly even dangerous—but I really liked him. And I liked having a big brother. "I don't know where he is. Back in New York, probably."

I heard the door open and looked up to see Alisa Soto, one of the newer members of our coven. She was a sophomore with thick golden brown hair and dark eyes that were so large, she appeared almost owlish. "Hi, everyone," she said shyly. She looked at me uncertainly. "Hey, Morgan."

"Hi," I replied, pleased to see her. She was younger than the rest of us and usually hung out with the other underclassmen before school. I guessed that her appearance meant she was finally—after weeks—starting to relax around us.

Sharon gave Alisa a bright smile and patted the space beside her. Alisa walked down to sit next to Sharon, murmuring hello to Bree and Robbie along the way.

Robbie glanced at his watch. "I've got to get to the library," he said. Bree released him reluctantly. "I've got to grab these last ten minutes to study before Spanish."

"I'll come with you," Bree said quickly.

An odd look flickered across Robbie's face, but just as soon as it had come, it was gone. "Great," he said. "Let's go. Later, guys." He waved and headed up the stairs.

Bree reached out and squeezed my arm. "We'll talk at lunch, okay? I want to hear all the details."

"Sure," I said. I watched, puzzled, as she turned and trotted after Robbie. It struck me as odd that Bree wanted to go with Robbie instead of hanging out with the rest of us. It wasn't really Bree's style to seek out extra study time.

"So Morgan, did you study for the test?" Jenna asked, slipping into Robbie's seat.

My stomach dropped. "Test?" I asked.

Jenna bit her lip. "You've got Powell, right?" she asked. "I thought he was giving all of his sections a test on the Civil War today."

It came back to me with sudden vividness and I groaned. "I thought that was *next* Thursday," I said. I was totally screwed.

Jenna touched my arm. "What period do you have history?" she asked.

"Fifth."

"Great—that's not until after lunch," she said reassuringly. "I'll give you my notes on the reading and you can study them then, along with your class notes." She dug in her backpack and pulled out the notes. "Here," she said, handing them over. "Don't worry, it's going to be fine."

I really had no choice but to try to believe her. "Thanks," I said as the first bell rang. I had the feeling it was going to be a very long day.

By the time I slid into my 1971 Plymouth Valiant—affectionately nicknamed Das Boot—my arms were practically shaking with exhaustion. I'd hidden Jenna's notes behind my textbook in every class. Unfortunately, the cramming hadn't helped. I'd wanted to tell Mr. Powell not to bother grading my exam. I knew I'd flunked.

I turned the key in the ignition and smiled as it turned over immediately. Old reliable. Mary K. was at cheerleading practice and had told me she'd catch a ride with one of her friends. It was the only thing she'd said to me all day.

Suddenly I didn't want to go home. I could picture myself all alone in the quiet house. My parents wouldn't be home for hours, and I had no one to talk to about my horrible day. Not that I *wanted* to tell my parents about flunking a test.

I started for Hunter's house. Please be home, I thought, remembering the sense of calm I'd felt with him the night before.

Hunter was standing in the front doorway as I pulled into his driveway, gravel crunching beneath my tires.

"Rough day?" he asked, leaning in to kiss me as I climbed the front steps.

"Horrendous." I wrapped my arms around his neck. His lips tasted like cinnamon tea.

He smiled. "Why don't you come in and tell me about it?"

The warm scent of cinnamon wafted past my nose as we stepped into the worn, comfortable living room. I knew without casting out my senses that Sky, Hunter's cousin, was upstairs.

"Should I say hello?" I asked.

Hunter hesitated. "I think she'll come down if she feels like it. She's been pretty low lately."

I nodded. Sky and Raven had been a couple for a while, but they'd recently broken up—thanks mostly to my half brother Killian. I wasn't sure how Raven felt—it was hard to break through her tough-girl exterior—but I knew Sky was in a lot of pain. I felt a pang of sympathy as I imagined Sky going through a breakup halfway around the world from most of her friends.

I shrugged off my coat. Hunter took it and hung it up next to his in the hall closet. Then he came and pulled me down beside him on the threadbare couch.

"I spoke with Eoife again this morning," he said. "She's concerned about you. She would like for you to learn more about magickal defenses, and so would I."

"What's that?" I asked. "Like, self-defense for witches or something?"

Hunter nodded without humor. "That's exactly what it

is." His green eyes seemed to deepen in color as he added, "Given your history, Morgan, it seems like a good thing for you to study. Also, it's one of the topics covered in the preinitiation rites."

"I thought I would be initiated as a witch a year and a day from the time of my first circle. I didn't realize I had to prepare for it."

"You don't," Hunter said. "That's a simple ceremony. I'm talking about your initiation as a blood witch, which isn't so simple. Once you're initiated into the coven, then you begin preparing for your preapprentice rites, which are a series of magickal power and knowledge tests. They're supposed to screen out blood witches who aren't yet serious enough or in tune with their power enough for apprenticeships." I stifled a groan at the thought of more tests as Hunter went on, "Once you pass those rites, you'll be paired as an apprentice with a blood witch who will guide you until you're ready for the full blood witch initiation."

"How long will that take?"

Hunter shrugged. "It depends," he said. "A few years."

I struggled to hide my disappointment. A few *years?*

"Anyway," Hunter said. "Eoife has found someone who can come here to tutor you in magickal defenses for two weeks. She's going to stay with Sky and me. Her name is Erin Murphy, and she'll be here this weekend."

"Is she good?" I asked.

"The best," he said. In his clipped English accent, the statement seemed to leave no room for doubt. "In the meantime Eoife asked me to show you the basics." He stood up and crossed the room. There was a dinged-up sideboard along the wall leading to the kitchen, and Hunter pulled out a small bronze dish and a piece of chalk. He drew a small circle on the floor on the other side of the coffee table. I stepped inside, and he drew the last piece closed. Then he took a pinch of salt from the dish and sprinkled it around the circle. "With this salt I purify our circle," he said.

We joined hands, closed our eyes, and breathed deeply for a few moments. With every breath I could feel my senses expanding. It was as if I was growing and reaching out, as if the house and everything in it was a living, breathing extension of myself. I felt myself draw power from the breath, and I sensed that Hunter was drawing the same power. Our bodies, joined at the fingertips, had become one, lost in the connection we felt with everything around us, including each other. Then we both dropped hands and found ourselves staring into each other's eyes.

It was as if a window opened, and I could see the true depths of Hunter's emotions—his fierce sense of protection, his trustworthiness, his love for me, and his appreciation for our connection. I also saw harsh and unyielding anger, and I knew that what I was seeing was the rage Hunter felt at what the dark forces had done to his family. Hunter's parents, pursued by the dark wave, had left him at a young age. I saw that Hunter believed they were still alive and that he could help them. I also saw his frustration at not being able to do more, his stubborn belief that if only he tried hard enough, he could put everything right. I saw these things, and I sucked in my breath.

Suddenly the window closed, and he was simply Hunter again.

"The first lesson is in something called tàth meànma divagnth," he explained.

"Is that like tàth meànma brach?" I asked, recalling the ceremony that I still thought of as the "Wiccan mind meld." Tàth meànma was a ritual through which two people could look into each other's minds and share thoughts, memories, beliefs. Tàth meànma brach was a sort of turbocharged version of regular tàth meànma, in which you exchanged basically everything that was in your brains. Alyce Fernbrake, a blood witch who ran an occult bookstore called Practical Magick, had gone through the ceremony with me.

"Not exactly," Hunter said. "The object of the divagnth is to use someone's power and divert it so that it can't hurt you."

"So it's sort of like witch tae kwon do?"

Hunter smiled. Then he grabbed my wrist lightly with his right hand and pointed to the wall with his left. I felt a quick rush through my body, as if I had touched an electric current. A sizzling bolt of blue fire exploded from Hunter's left index finger. It hit the wall and dissolved harmlessly.

I felt dizzy and struggled to suck oxygen into my lungs. "Are you all right?" Hunter asked, placing his hands on my hips.

I took a few deep breaths. "Yeah, but it kind of knocks the wind out of you."

Hunter nodded. "It can be very effective when you're dealing with an enemy." His voice was grim, and as I felt his strong hands on my hips, I realized yet again that Hunter had years of training and knowledge that I could hardly even begin to imagine.

I looked him in the eye. "Teach me," I said.

Hunter spent the better part of an hour showing me different techniques for deflecting power. Although he claimed that these were pretty basic self-defense moves, all of them were completely unknown to me. It was fascinating to realize that—even with all of Alyce's knowledge, which was considerable—there were entire worlds left to learn.

"Excellent work," Hunter said as I used one of his blocks.

Now that the energy wasn't flying around the room, I felt the exhaustion of the day settle on me like a heavy blanket. Hunter touched my hair. "Should I take you home?" he asked.

"No," I said quickly. I definitely didn't want to go home now. "Maybe . . . maybe we could go to a movie?" I suggested.

Sky came down the stairs. She was naturally fair but looked even paler than usual. "Hello, Sky," I said.

"Oh, hello, Morgan," Sky said, looking surprised. "I didn't realize you were here." That struck me as odd. Sky was a powerful blood witch. She should have sensed my presence. But as I looked at her drawn face, it was pretty clear that she was off in her own world. "Am I interrupting?" she asked, glancing from my face to Hunter's.

"I'm just trying to talk Hunter into going to a movie," I said. "There's a—a great new foreign film playing at the Pavilion," I said. Actually, what was playing there was an action adventure I'd been dying to see that I knew Hunter would never go for. But it was made in Hong Kong—that made it foreign, right? "It's still early," I went on, glancing at the clock on the mantel. It was only six-fifteen. "We can grab a slice of pizza before the movie and I can still be home by

ten." I put on my best overeager face and batted my eyelashes.

Hunter laughed and gave in. "All right," he said, holding
up his hands.

"Great!" I rushed to the kitchen to use his phone while
Sky wandered back upstairs. I punched in the number for my
house and listened as it rang a few times and the machine
picked up. I left a message explaining that I was going to a
movie with Hunter. Considering the way my parents had
reacted to him last night, I figured they'd be okay with me
spending some quality time with him. At least, until I got my
history grade.

Hunter and I grabbed a quick slice at Pino's Pizza, then
drove over to the theater. When we walked up to the
ticket window, Hunter said, "Two for *Fire Dragons,* please." I
gaped at him as he pulled out his wallet. He noticed the
look on my face, and the corners of his mouth twitched up
into a smile. "What?" he said. "You didn't actually think you
had me fooled with that line about going to see a foreign
film, did you?"

I laughed and shook my head. The more I felt I knew
Hunter, the more capable he was of surprising me.

The wind was blowing my hair around my face, and I
pushed it back with both hands as we walked inside. The
Pavilion used to be a real theater, the kind where you see
plays and stuff, and the interior is decorated with images
from Greek myths. I always liked to sit in the front of the
balcony because the view is great and hardly anyone likes to
sit there but me.

We made a quick stop at the concession stand for a

medium popcorn and a Diet Coke for me. When I turned around, I came face-to-face with Bree and Robbie.

"Hey, guys," Robbie said. He pulled a few kernels from the top of my bag of popcorn and stuffed them in his mouth.

"Watch it," I joked. "Do you know how much that popcorn costs?"

"I'll pay you back," Robbie promised, and placed his order for a large popcorn and two sodas.

"And a box of Raisinets," Bree added. I smiled at her.

The blond girl gathered their order and lined everything up on the counter. As she was ringing their total, she said shyly, "Robbie?"

Robbie gave her a blank look. "Yes?"

The girl blushed. "I'm Jessica Watts . . . from Mrs. Carleson's class? Fifth grade? You sat next to me."

"Jessica Watts?" Robbie repeated. He sounded shocked.

I felt my own mouth drop open. Jessica Watts? I thought. As in "Mega Watts"? Bree and I had been in Mrs. Norton's class in the fifth grade, while Robbie was across the hall with Mrs. Carleson. The classes didn't really mix much, but Jessica Watts had been famous at our school. At the age of ten she had already weighed over 150 pounds. She got teased a lot and bullied because of her weight. Now it looked like she had lost thirty pounds—and grown four inches. She looked great.

"Wow, Jessica," Robbie said, "you look *terrific!* I don't know if you remember Bree and Morgan," he went on, waving a hand at us. "They went to Widow's Vale Elementary, too. And this is Hunter Niall," he added.

"Hey," I said.

"Hi," Bree said, checking her watch. "Robbie, the movie's going to start in five minutes."

Robbie looked at her. For a minute I expected him to protest, but instead he just said, "Yeah, okay. We'd better find a seat. Great to see you, Jessica."

Jessica grinned. "See you around."

As we stepped away from the counter, Robbie was still shaking his head. "God, I can't believe how great Jessica looks," he said.

Bree snorted impatiently. "She went on a diet—big deal."

"Bree!" I tossed a kernel of popcorn at her. She batted it away with annoyance.

Robbie gave Bree a look. "I'm not just talking about the weight," he insisted. "Back in fifth grade, Jessica always looked like a dog who was expecting to get kicked. She looks so much more confident now. . . ." His voice trailed off, but I knew what he meant, and he was right.

Bree didn't answer, and I wondered why. She usually had an opinion to voice. I glanced at her sideways and noticed her fiddling with one strand of her dark, perfectly tousled hair. I had known Bree a long time, since we were little kids, and I knew what that gesture meant. She was worried.

But what about? I wondered. It wasn't like Bree to get jealous or possessive. In fact, Bree had a history of never letting any guy get too close. She had left a string of love casualties in her wake. I decided to ask her later what was up. Bree didn't have the world's greatest family life. I wondered whether everything was okay with her.

"Are you two heading up to the balcony?" Bree asked as we neared the foot of the stairs.

"Yup. Want to come?" I teased, knowing what the answer would be. We'd been having the same debate since the seventh grade.

"Forget it," Bree replied. "You know how I feel about that rickety old railing."

"See you guys later, then," Robbie said.

Bree and Robbie walked through the main entrance while Hunter and I headed up the side stairs. I smiled as we walked down the aisle to my favorite seats in the front of the balcony. Looking down on the theater below, I saw that there were quite a few heads in the main part. But the balcony was completely empty. We settled into our seats just as the opening credits began to roll. Hunter put his arm along the back of my seat and I leaned against him, feeling like a corny couple out of the 1950s.

"What's this movie about, anyway?" Hunter whispered as the title flashed across the screen in letters of flame.

"A bunch of guys kicking butt," I replied.

"Ah. Lovely." Hunter settled back against his chair.

About twenty minutes into the movie, I began to notice that he seemed uncomfortable. He shifted left, then right, then took his arm away from the back of my seat and gripped the armrest.

"Are you okay?" I whispered. Hunter didn't answer. I turned to look at him and gasped. His face, reflected in the strange shadows of the flickering movie screen, was dead white, and his mouth was opening and closing as if he was trying to speak but couldn't form the words. My heart pounded as Hunter squeezed his eyes shut and sucked in his breath. I grabbed his arm and was nearly crushed by the weight of some unseen force. Wave after wave of emotions flooded over me—despair, agony, longing, regret, fear. Deep fear. The sensations were so strong that I thought they would overwhelm me as they ripped through my body.

Then suddenly the flood of feelings stopped. Hunter sank down listlessly in his seat. It was over.

I flopped back against my chair, exhausted, and listened to the sound of Hunter's breathing—or was it my own? We were both inhaling in ragged gasps.

"What happened?" I whispered.

Hunter was pale, and his chest was still heaving. "It was my father," he said softly.

Cold fingers of dread crept up my spine. "Are you sure?" I asked in a hushed voice. Hunter's father and mother had disappeared when Hunter was a child. In an effort to save themselves and their family, they'd placed their children with relatives and gone into hiding, running from the dark wave. Hunter hadn't heard from them in years . . . until recently, when he'd received a scrying message that he felt certain was from his father. The meaning of the message was still unclear, but Hunter had sent a spelled seed pod down the Hudson River in the hope that he might make contact. But until now there had been no word, and I knew that Hunter feared the worst.

"I'm positive," he replied.

"But—what does it mean?" I asked.

Hunter sat forward, leaning his elbows against his knees. He stayed there a moment, hunched over in that position, as though completely drained. Finally he faced me. "I don't know what it means," he said, "but I'm going to find out."

I exhaled a long breath, trying to release the last of the fear and tension. I looked up at the movie screen. Its flickering images suddenly seemed like nonsense. "Let's get out of here," I whispered.

Hunter was already out of his seat by the time I finished my sentence.

I spent the drive back thinking about Hunter's message, wondering what it could mean. A glance over at Hunter showed me that his jaw was clenched and he was concentrating on the road. I watched the dark, hulking forms of trees flicker past the car windows, and I thought about what it must be like to know that your parents are out there somewhere. To know that they may need your help. And to be unable to give it.

Soon Hunter's battered Honda was gliding to a stop in front of his house. He shifted into neutral and stared straight ahead for a moment. Then wordlessly he swung open his car door and stepped out into the frigid night. I did the same, following him toward Das Boot. I would drive home from here.

Hunter was staring out into the darkness. I didn't feel ready to say good night. "Hunter," I began, but my voice trailed off. I didn't know what to say. I leaned in close and wrapped my arms around him, wishing I could just hold him and make it better.

"I'm going to find them," Hunter said simply. For a moment the words seemed to hang there, coiling around us in the quiet night air. Then he pulled away and turned to me, his green eyes glinting in the dimness with a strange, almost predatory look.

"How?" I asked.

"I'm not sure," Hunter said. "The council was supposed to pursue a few leads, but they haven't had any new information in a long time. They told me not to act, but I think I've waited long enough. The time has come to step in myself."

"But you have no idea where they are!" I protested.

Hunter shrugged. "Not yet," he said. Then his gaze seemed to soften, and he looked into my eyes. He leaned over, and his lips met mine. His kiss was gentle but insistent, and I felt my heart race at his touch. His fingers felt beneath my jacket and traced along my back. I shivered and pulled away from him.

"Hunter," I said, "I know I sound like a goofy movie girl-friend, but will you please just promise that you'll be careful?"

He hesitated before finally shaking his head. "I'll be as careful as I can."

I thought about the dark wave, about what it might take to rescue Hunter's parents. He was right—*careful* wasn't a word that would go very far in helping them. "All right," I said finally, fighting the wave of fear that I felt. It would have to be good enough. "I'll be thinking about you tonight." I gave him one final kiss, then swung open my car door and slid onto the seat.

"Good night, Morgan." Hunter turned, and his form retreated up the walk to his front door. I watched him until he went inside. Then I drove home, alone with my thoughts. I wished I understood what had happened. Memories of the violent emotions I'd felt swirled through my mind until I reached my house.

The hallway was silent when I went inside. I shrugged off my coat and hung it on a peg, then pulled off my boots so that I wouldn't track mud all over the house.

"Hi, Mom," I said, walking into the brightly lit kitchen. She was hunched over a pile of paperwork at the kitchen table. I pulled a glass out of the cabinet.

"Getting in a little late, aren't you?" my mom remarked.

I stopped, confused. We'd left the movie early. "Didn't you get my message?" I asked. "I was at the Pavilion with Hunter."

"I got your message," my mom replied. "But Morgan, you know it's a school night. Have you finished your homework?"

I hesitated but couldn't lie. "No," I admitted.

My mother heaved an exasperated sigh. "Well, I don't think I need to explain what my problem with that is," she said. Her frown etched deep lines around her mouth, making her look older and tired. "Or do I? I don't know, Morgan, lately I feel like your priorities have shifted."

"That's not true," I protested.

"Isn't it?" my mother asked. She looked even more weary, and there was a catch in her voice as she added, "You never join us at church anymore. I feel like we hardly see you—like you're just disappearing from this family."

I suddenly realized why my mother had been so eager to get to know Hunter. It wasn't just because she wanted to make sure that he was a decent person—it was because she felt like I was slipping away, and she wanted to bring me back. "Mom, I'm sorry," I said, feeling a wave of guilt. "I guess I shouldn't have stayed out late on a school night. I just thought that you and Dad liked Hunter so much, you wouldn't mind. And I don't have a lot of homework tonight. I can still finish."

"Morgan, I don't want to force you to do things you don't want to do." My mom pushed away her paperwork and looked at me. "And I do like Hunter. But I miss you. We all do. I'd like to find a way to make sure that we can spend some time together."

I thought for a moment. "Maybe we could have a regular night to get together," I suggested. "A family night or something."

My mom pursed her lips a moment and folded her arms across her chest, her thinking pose. "Well, maybe we could do something like that once a week."

I nodded, thinking that maybe, if we spent more time together, my parents might realize that it was possible for me to have both them *and* Wicca in my life.

"Okay," my mom said finally. "I'll check with Dad and Mary K., and we'll set up a regular night." She leaned over and kissed me on the forehead. "I'll think of something fun we can do together."

I grabbed an apple from the bowl on the table. "Sounds good. I'm going upstairs to do my problem set. Sorry I was so late," I said. Eyeing her paperwork, I added, "And don't work too hard."

"Mmm." My mom bent over her papers again.

Biting into the apple, I went upstairs and crawled onto my bed with my calculus book. But the minute I got settled on my down comforter, the wave of exhaustion I'd been holding back all day washed over me with full force. I closed my eyes, intending to rest them for just a minute. I didn't wake up until morning.

3.
Attack

Okay, Time for another entry in my "Book of Shadows." I feel kind of silly calling This wire-bound notebook by such an imposing-sounding name. "Book of Shadows" is supposed To be for spells and chants and stuff like That—and I don't really know any. Still, both Hunter and Sky Think we should keep one, and everyone else in Kithic seems To do it. So I got one. Which means That I have a special place To share my "wonderful" news.

Dad is marrying Hilary. She's pregnant. And moving in with us in a few weeks.

I Tried really hard To act happy for Dad, but he didn't ask me how I felt about it. So I guess he didn't really want To know.

As I write This, my mother's picture is looking at me from my dresser across The room. I wonder what she would Think of all This. I honestly have no idea—I barely knew her. She died when I was Three. I like To Think That she'd be glad my father is happy with someone new. I like To Think ThaT she was a nicer person Than I am.

Hilary is coming over laTer. I'm glad I won'T be around, I'm going To circle. I have To admiT ThaT when Bree firsT asked if I wanTed To join KiThic, I wasn'T so sure ThaT iT was a good idea. BuT aT The very firsT circle we held hands and Sky TaughT us how To feel each oTher's energy. IT was Truly magickal, The kind of experience you can'T puT inTo words. I felT myself opening up like a flower. ThaT's The besT Thing abouT The coven. In a weird way—I don'T really undersTand iT myself— iT's almosT like coming home.

Bree jusT called To Tell me she's going To be abouT Ten minuTes laTe To pick me up. She's giving Morgan a ride, Too. I know iT's dumb, buT Morgan makes me uncomforTable. She has magickal powers. Of course, everyone else in The coven Thinks iT's incredibly cool. One Time she made flowers appear ouT of Thin air. I had To look around aT everyone else and Tell myself, "IT's all right. Nobody else is scared." Then I focused on my breaThing To calm myself.

I know ThaT magick is a parT of Wicca, and The smaller spells—using herbs and oils To heal, channeling your energy Toward someThing you wanT To achieve— Those seem beauTiful To me, buT Morgan's magick is differenT. IT feels dangerous, ouT of conTrol. And even her own sisTer is afraid of iT.

BuT ThaT doesn'T mean ThaT I shouldn'T drive To circle wiTh Morgan or even ThaT she isn'T a nice person. RighT?

—Alisa

"You look gorgeous," I told Bree as I ducked into her BMW, Breezy, on Saturday evening. She wore a soft-looking gray coat over black wool pants and managed to look sleek, sophisticated, and sexy all at once.

"Thanks," Bree said without enthusiasm.

"So," I said, "will Robbie be at the circle?" I actually already knew the answer to this—Robbie and I had chatted for about one second that afternoon before Mrs. Fiorello, my mom's coworker, had beeped in on the other line and I'd had to hand the phone over to my mom. But I was looking for an opening. In fact, I'd asked Bree for a ride especially so I could talk to her.

"Yeah, he'll be there." There was an odd note in her voice. My opening.

"Is everything okay with you guys?" I asked as nonchalantly as I could.

"What do you mean?" Bree's voice was taut, like a piano wire.

"I don't know, you just seem to be . . . not yourself lately." I gripped the door handle, preparing for an attack. Bree could be prickly about personal comments.

She sighed. "Yeah," she said, and her voice trailed off into the darkness. The road hummed beneath us, and for a moment I thought that she wasn't going to say anything else. "I've been feeling—I don't know." Bree shook her head, as if frustrated that the thoughts wouldn't form a cohesive sentence for her. "I guess I've been feeling kind of *possessive*." She laughed. "Pretty weird, huh?"

"For you? Um, yeah," I agreed. "You usually run for the hills when someone acts possessive with you."

"Tell me about it." Bree scowled. "I just can't seem to stop myself. It's just—I've never felt this way about a guy before."

"But that's great," I said. "It means you care."

"Maybe." Bree sounded doubtful. "I've never really let myself get this close to someone before. I guess this is why." Running an impatient hand through her dark hair, she added, "I really hate the way I'm feeling right now, Morgan. I hate the way I'm acting. I don't want to be clingy and needy—but I just don't want to let Robbie out of my sight. I guess I'm just worried that he's going to get bored with me or something. That now that I actually care about someone, he's going to move on."

I reached over and grabbed Bree's hand. Even through our gloves, I could feel her hand radiating heat. "That's not going to happen," I assured her. "Robbie is nuts about you. He's been nuts about you for a long time—and that's not going to change." I pictured Robbie in my mind, remembering how he'd confessed to me his feelings for Bree. "Besides, he'd never want to hurt you."

Bree squeezed my hand. There was a catch in her voice as she said, "I know."

I leaned my head against the cool passenger-side window. I wanted to say more, but we were almost at Alisa's house, and I didn't want to discuss this in front of her. My breath made a steamy crescent on the side of the window, and I remembered the two of us in elementary school, breathing on the cold glass of the school bus window and writing our names in the steam. That was before Bree's mom moved away to live with her boyfriend in Europe. It was before her older brother,

Ty, went off to college and before Bree's corporate-lawyer father began working so hard that she hardly ever saw him anymore. Bree was so beautiful and poised, it was easy to forget that her life was sort of lonely. Until now, she'd always kept the guys she dated at a safe distance. But Robbie was different—they'd been friends before they started going out, and he knew her too well to be satisfied with staying at arm's length. He was chipping away at the wall that surrounded her. I wondered whether it would open her up to caring about people in a new way or whether it might make her crumble.

I briefly considered talking to Robbie about what was going on with Bree but rejected the thought. It was their relationship, after all. Instead I asked her, "Have you spoken to Robbie about this?"

"No," she admitted.

"Maybe you should."

Bree bit her lip and didn't reply. She made a left turn. The silence yawned between us as we pulled up into the circular driveway in front of a small, tidy ranch-style house. Alisa must have been watching for us because a moment later she hurried out the front door.

Bree turned to me. "Okay, I'll talk to him," she said quickly.

Good, I thought. I'd done my good deed for the day.

Alisa said a shy hello, and Bree eased the car back onto the road toward Hunter's house. The car was silent for the rest of the drive. I guess we were all lost in our own thoughts.

Hunter's small living room was already filling up by the time we arrived. The room was lit by the warm glow of candles, and in the soft light the worn furniture seemed comfortable and welcoming. The air was heavy with the scent of mulling spices—Sky must have put a pot of cider on the stove. Robbie stood in the corner, talking to Simon Bakehouse, but the minute we walked in, he flashed Bree an enormous grin and hurried over. I gave Bree an I-told-you-so look, and she smiled as Robbie draped an arm around her shoulders. They melted into the rear of the room.

From his place by the tattered armchair, Hunter waved to me and continued an intense-looking conversation with Sky. Jenna came over and said hello to me, and she and I chatted for a few minutes. "Are you feeling all right?" I asked.

"My asthma's bothering me," she admitted. "I took a shot off my inhaler before I came here, but it hasn't helped much."

I resisted the urge to lay my hands on her back. I'd helped her with her asthma before. But I knew that Hunter and Sky frowned on such practices, and I was trying to show them that I'd turned over a new leaf.

Not everyone had arrived yet, so I headed to the kitchen to help myself to cider. When I pushed open the door, I was surprised to see Alisa sitting alone at the small table, staring off into space. I hesitated a moment, reluctant to barge in on her. But I decided it would look weird to scurry away, so I just plowed ahead.

"Hey," I said, crossing to the stove. Someone had put out some plastic foam cups on the countertop so people could help themselves to the cider. "This smells great—do you want some?"

"Hmm?" Alisa jumped slightly. "Oh—no. Thanks." She tried to smile at me, but she looked tired . . . and something else. Sad, maybe.

I pulled out a chair and sat next to her. I took a slow sip

of cider and felt its warmth spread through me, chasing away the February chill. I wondered why Alisa was in here alone. "Is everything okay?" I asked finally. I felt awkward. I really didn't know Alisa that well. Normally I didn't like to pry into people's lives, but there was something about Alisa that made me feel oddly protective, almost like she was a vulnerable younger sister or something.

Surprise flickered over her face. For a moment it seemed like she wanted to tell me what was on her mind. Almost instantly, though, she seemed to think better of it, and her face closed. "I've just had some weird news, that's all," she said. She looked down at the table.

Before I could decide whether to press her for details, the kitchen door swung open to reveal Sky. Her pale skin and fair hair seemed to glow against the midnight blue linen shirt she was wearing. "Morgan, Alisa," she said, "we're getting ready to start."

Stepping into the living room, I saw that Hunter had already drawn a circle on the floor. Alisa and I stepped into it behind Sky. I tried to move toward Hunter but found myself almost directly across the circle from him. Once everyone had settled down, I was surprised to see someone new next to Sky. She looked young and was about five feet tall, with dark red hair and green eyes. Her slim figure made her seem coltish, as if she were about to go through a growth spurt. I wondered who she was.

"Everyone, before we begin, I'd like to introduce our guest," Sky said. "This is Erin Murphy."

Erin Murphy. I knew that name. Erin Murphy was the witch who was coming to teach me magickal defenses. But this couldn't be her! I studied Erin's face more closely and saw faint creases around her mouth and eyes. Maybe she's older than she looks, I thought. Automatically I reached out with my senses and felt her power. She was strong. Really strong.

Erin had been looking at Sky, but her eyes suddenly flicked to me. The steady gaze felt like a hand against my forehead, but after a moment the pressure stopped, and she smiled. I resisted the urge to rub my temples.

"Erin is a healer from Scotland," Sky went on. She didn't say anything to the rest of the coven about the fact that Erin was a magickal defense expert.

Jenna looked hopeful, and I knew that she was thinking about her asthma. From her place next to me, Alisa shuffled uneasily. "A healer?" she repeated.

"You think I'm not old enough to know what I'm doing? I'm forty-seven," Erin said abruptly, turning her sharp eyes on Alisa. I guess she was used to people's confusion about her age. Then her face took on a curious expression as she still looked at Alisa.

Alisa blushed to the roots of her hair. She blinked uncomfortably and brought her hand to her forehead. "I didn't mean—"

"It's quite all right," Erin cut her off in a musical brogue. "If you can believe it, the stewardess on my flight over asked me if my ma would be meetin' me at the gate." Laughter rippled through the circle, and I felt everyone relax. Erin studied Alisa a moment longer, then smiled. I glanced across the circle at Hunter, and he grinned at me.

"You don't sound Scottish," Matt Adler said.

"I'm an immigrant," Erin said, and something about her

tone made everyone chuckle again. "I'm Irish, living in Scotland. On vacation in America." She looked around the circle, and her eyes landed on me. "Any other questions?" she asked. Her tone was playful but seemed to hold a challenge as well. I had a million questions, but I felt too shy to ask them. I could practically feel the power rolling off this woman.

After a moment Sky took out some salt and began to purify the circle. Raven had managed to maneuver herself so that she was between Sky and Matt, whom she'd fooled around with a few times back in the fall. I wondered how Sky would react.

Sky began placing incense for air, sand for earth, a candle for fire, and a small cup of water at various points on the circle. I could see that the line of her jaw was rigid, although she was making an effort to seem unaffected by Raven's presence. It was actually kind of strange to see the two of them next to each other. Raven had clearly taken more care than usual with her appearance tonight—she was wearing a red velvet peasant blouse that laced up the front and black leather pants. Her dyed black hair cascaded down her back. She looked like a biker-chick version of Lady Guinevere. She was dark and lush, fire to Sky's ice.

Sky set down the last bowl and returned to her place in the circle. Hunter looked up at me. "There's a full moon tonight—very auspicious," he said. "Let's join hands and walk deasil." I was standing between Alisa and Robbie, and I was glad for Robbie's familiar presence as we all began to move clockwise around the room. As the group moved together, I could feel the energy build around me. I remembered the way it used to press in on me when I'd first begun coming to circles, and I was glad that I was now more in control of the magick that surrounded me. Now the power seemed wonderful and exhilarating, without the edge of fear that it used to hold.

"In Wicca we aren't afraid to ask the Goddess for what we need," Sky said. "When you feel it, make a wish. During a full moon it may very well be granted."

Next to me Robbie was the first to speak. "I wish for endurance."

On the other side of him Bree said, "I wish for peace."

Ethan went next. "I wish for strength," he said. He cast a quick look at Sharon, who was standing next to him.

Sharon met his look. "I wish for understanding."

We went around the circle, and everyone said what they wished for. It was kind of interesting. Everyone wished for intangible things.

Finally it was Alisa's turn. "I wish things could stay the way they are," she said quietly. There was a sadness in her voice that tugged at my heart.

I glanced across the circle at Hunter, and my mind flashed back to the kiss we'd shared a few nights ago. That was a moment I'd wanted to preserve perfectly, like a leaf in amber. But things change—that's their nature. I felt a wave of sympathy for Alisa, for her doomed wish. I squeezed her hand.

Hunter gave me a nod, and I knew it was my turn. I racked my brain for something to say, and I suddenly remembered the first circle I'd ever been to. Everyone had named something they wanted to banish. I'd said I wanted to banish limitations. In the weeks that followed, my life had opened up. I'd found Wicca, I'd discovered the truth about my heritage, and my power had started to reveal itself. But now, finally, my world seemed to be settling down, and I was growing comfortable with who I was.

"I wish to learn my limits," I said. I felt Alisa turn toward me, but when I faced her, she had already turned away. I wondered at my own choice of words. In order to learn my limits, I would have to test them. How much further would I have to go?

We continued walking deasil for a moment, then we all stopped and threw our hands up. "That was good," Sky said. Her cheeks were flushed pink, and I knew that she was feeling the same energy I was. "Let's take it down." We all sat on the floor.

"I feel a little dizzy," Alisa whispered as she crossed her legs.

I nodded. We had been moving in the circle for quite a while, building up a lot of energy. I was glad to be sitting, too.

Sky reached out and picked up the cream-colored pillar candle that represented fire. With a gentle breath she extinguished the flame and set the candle in the center of the circle. Smoke curled toward the ceiling as Sky said, "Morgan, please light this."

I frowned. I could only assume that Sky was hoping to demonstrate my magick to Erin, but reluctance swelled in my chest. Most of my friends in the coven had no idea that I could light fires with my mind, and I wasn't really keen on them finding out. I loved my power, but I'd seen the gulf it had created between me and Robbie, and, in another way, between me and Bree. I was something different. I didn't want my friends to fear me.

Hunter looked at me with serious eyes. I could tell that he wanted me to light the candle, too. Erin leaned forward slightly, one eyebrow arched, almost as if she doubted I could do it.

The circle was hushed and still. A feeling of expectancy filled the room.

I faced the candle and quieted my mind. The energy that still curled through the room flowed through me, and in a moment the wick sputtered and burst into flame. A few people gasped. Alisa's eyes flew wide, and she drew her knees toward her chest and leaned away from the candle, as if it were a snake that might bite her.

"Oh my *God*, Morgan," Bree said. She was staring at me.

The candle flame burned steadily, and I looked over it at Hunter. His face was golden in the soft glow.

Suddenly a frigid breeze blew through the room, as if someone had opened a window. The candle flame hissed and went out, then the candle itself toppled over, spilling wax on the carpet. An icy finger of fear tickled my scalp. That was a big candle, I thought. It shouldn't have blown over so easily.

A murmur ran through the room.

"What's happening?" Alisa whispered.

But before I could answer, the lightbulb in the lamp behind Hunter exploded with a loud *pop*. Someone screamed. For a moment I thought it was me, but then I realized it was Alisa. She stared at me in horror.

On the other side of the room the bookcase behind Hunter shuddered, and a book flew off the shelf, hurling itself against the opposite wall. Reflexively I threw up my hands as the entire shelf of books flew after the first one, landing on the wall with thud after vicious thud. The bulbs of the other three lamps exploded in rapid succession, the sound like gunfire. Hunter stood up and ran to the windows.

"Stop it!" Alisa screamed. "Stop it, Morgan!"

"I can't!" I shouted. I had no idea what was happening or what had caused it.

On Alisa's other side Sharon reached to pull her into a hug, but Alisa fought her off as the room was plunged into darkness. Hunter stepped away from the window, letting the cold moonlight trickle in. Alisa was still screaming. I could see Erin's small form as she stood up and began to chant.

Goddess, we trust in you to protect us,
With this prayer we banish fear.

It was a short chant, and as she said it over and over, Alisa's cries grew more faint until the only noise I heard was a faint sniffling. The rest of us took up the chant. There was strength in the simplicity of the words, and as I said them, I felt their magick working on me. I took deep breaths and imagined a white light growing inside me, and I tried to release the fear that had held me in its grip. After a few minutes the room felt calm again, although the warm energy from before had disappeared.

There was a light scraping sound, then a small burst of flame as Sky struck a match. Leaning forward, she stood the pillar candle up and lit it. Hunter, who was still standing, took the packet of matches from her and began lighting candles all around the room. I looked around the circle at everyone's faces. Robbie's lips were pressed tightly together, and I could feel anger flowing from him. Bree looked at me like she couldn't remember who I was, and Jenna stared at the floor, avoiding my eyes. Matt, Thalia Cutter, and Simon were wide-eyed, silent. Hunter and Sky were impassive, but Raven was gazing at me with what looked like respect. And Erin looked at me like I was a fascinating bug, something slightly revolting but nonetheless interesting.

"I didn't do anything," I said loudly. "That wasn't me."

Alisa shakily got to her feet. Sharon stood and put her arm around Alisa's shoulders. Alisa turned to her and asked, "Will you take me home?" She sounded very young. Sharon nodded, and Alisa turned toward the door. I tried not to feel hurt. I knew Alisa blamed me, but this *wasn't* my fault.

"I'm sorry, you guys," Sharon said. "But I think Alisa—"

"It's all right. Actually, why don't we call it a night?" Hunter said quietly. "We'll talk about this next week, when we've had a chance to sort it out."

"Right." Robbie got to his feet. He didn't look at me.

Bree peered around him. "Morgan—?"

"I'm staying," I said. "Hunter, you can take me home later, right?"

Hunter confirmed with a nod. In a few moments everyone had said their good-byes, and the house was empty except for Hunter, Sky, Erin, and me. The blood witches.

Sky extinguished the candles and we moved to the kitchen, where Hunter poked around, looking for new lightbulbs.

"Well, that was a very interesting circle," Erin said brightly as she pulled up a chair to the farmhouse table.

I ladled hot cider into four cups and handed them out. "What *happened?*" I asked as I warmed my hands on the sides of my cup.

"I was about to ask you that, my dear," Erin replied. She took a sip of her cider.

"It wasn't me," I said again, feeling resentful.

Erin put down her cup. Leaning forward on one arm, she looked at me closely. "Are you sure?" she asked. I opened my mouth to reply, but Erin held up a hand. "I'm not saying that you caused it on purpose. It might have been an accident." Leaning back in her chair, she added, "It was my understanding that there were only four blood witches here tonight. And only one who hasn't been trained. Or initiated. You."

"It wasn't me," I insisted. "I would have known if I were making something happen. I would have felt power flowing through me." I turned to Hunter. "Right?"

Hunter looked at Erin. "Morgan is extremely powerful," he said. "She may not be initiated, but she has gained a great deal of control over her magick."

Erin shrugged. "Perhaps," she said. I couldn't tell if she was convinced. "All right, then," she went on, turning to Sky, "what else might have caused it?"

Hunter and Sky exchanged glances. "Amyranth?" Sky asked. Hunter nodded, and I felt a tightening in my chest. Amyranth. Ciaran's coven. They had kidnapped me, tried to drain my power. Were they after me again?

Was . . . was Ciaran himself after me? I felt cold at the thought. I was more or less certain that he knew I'd worked with the council to try and trap him. He might want revenge. True, I was his daughter. His flesh and blood. He loved me— I really believed that. Then again, he had loved my mother. And that hadn't stopped him from killing her.

Erin cocked her head and thought for a moment. "There are sigils of protection on this house, I presume?"

"Yes, of course," Hunter said. "But I should redraw them."

Erin stood up. "Do that." She put a gentle hand on my shoulder. "Sky and I will do a few spells to protect Morgan herself."

I looked up at her in surprise, but she just continued to watch Hunter as he grabbed a flashlight and went out the back door. In a few moments we could hear his footsteps crunching through snow as he visited each window and door and retraced the runes of protection on them.

Erin took her chair again, and then she, Sky, and I joined hands around the table. Erin began to chant. Though I didn't understand them, the words sounded beautiful in her lilting voice. The energy flowed between us, and suddenly I felt filled with light, with magick. Serenity flowed around me.

After a few moments Erin let go. Picking up my hand, she traced a sigil on my palm, one I had never seen before.

"This will protect you." Her voice was strong and sure. I looked into her cool, clear eyes. She's a master of magickal defenses, I told myself. I can believe her.

Anyway, what choice did I have?

4.
The Vision

September 15, 1971

The sky is the color of steel today, and the bitter wind has begun to blow from the north. The flags are flying at half-mast, and there seems to be a hush over the town of Gloucester. We heard this morning that the <u>Lady Marie</u> went down in last night's storm.

All five fishermen aboard are believed dead—Captain James Dallman, Tim Flanagan, Arnold Jennings, Jason McGreevy, and Andrew Lewis. The storm came up so suddenly that the men on board weren't even able to radio for help. They sank fifty miles off Eastern Point.

They haven't found the bodies.

Sam has been quiet all day. He knew Andrew Lewis pretty well. We all did, actually—Drew grew up only two blocks from our house. He was two years older than I am and was a big baseball hero *in high school. He always let the little kids play in the neighborhood games and taught them how to field and bat. Sam looked up to him.*

Some people said that Drew should have tried for a career in baseball—he even got a college scholarship to play. But Drew just wanted to be a fisherman like his dad. He didn't want to leave Gloucester.

And now he's gone. Of course, that's the risk you take, being a fisherman. It's a dangerous job. Not even all the magick of Wicca can save you from the full force of a storm.

—Sarah Curtis

"Let me take you home." Hunter stood over me, worry etching fine lines around his mouth. "I've finished with the sigils. There isn't much else we can do tonight."

When I stood, I felt like every muscle in my body was aching. The night's tension had made me stiff.

Erin and Sky were talking together in the living room, and they both seemed subdued as we said good-bye. Still, there was something in Erin's gaze as she looked at me that seemed sharp and wary. I felt like I had spent the evening under a microscope. I was on edge until Hunter and I were safely tucked into his beat-up Honda. He turned the key in the ignition, and we were off.

As we neared a heavily wooded dip in the road, the fog grew thicker and Hunter had to slow the car. My senses snapped to alert. The road revealed itself only a yard at a time, and deer were known to dart out onto the asphalt. It could be very dangerous.

Hunter slowed even further as we headed into a curve that I knew all too well. It was here, almost two months before, that Cal had suddenly reappeared after he and his mother had left Widow's Vale. It had been a dark night like this one, and Cal had been standing right in the middle of the road. At the memory, the hair on the back of my neck began to prickle, and without even realizing it, I cast out my senses.

I felt nothing. I exhaled slowly, trying to calm myself. There's nothing here, I told myself. Focus on your breathing and calm down. Another deep inhale and Hunter was easing around the curve, beginning to accelerate slightly. I felt better.

Just then, Hunter slammed on the brakes and the car swerved sickeningly.

Someone was standing in the middle of the road.

"Cal!" An involuntary cry escaped me.

Goddess, help me, I thought desperately. Hunter muttered curses and fought with the steering wheel. I felt the jarring pressure of the seat belt across my chest as we came to a sudden skidding stop and I was thrown forward in my seat. We were half on, half off the shoulder.

I turned to make sure Hunter was okay and saw that his eyes were huge. He was staring straight ahead, still gripping the steering wheel. In front of us, the figure in the fog had not moved.

I stared at it, my lips moving dumbly for a moment before I realized that it wasn't Cal—at least, not in any incarnation I knew. The figure had a human form, but it was shadowy and indistinct. It looked vaguely female. Who—or what—was it?

I leaned forward to look at it more closely and saw that

it seemed to be part of the mist—as if the fog itself were struggling to come to life. For a moment I thought it was an optical illusion, a trick of mist and light, but then the figure actually turned and looked directly at us. Its eyes seemed to see, and it gazed at us mournfully. Sadness gripped me with iron claws. Holding my breath, I didn't dare to look away.

I reached for Hunter's hand and found that it was icy. After a long moment the figure disappeared.

"What was that?" I whispered.

Hunter didn't respond. Instead he merely closed his eyes, and I knew that he was pouring every ounce of concentration he had into casting out his senses. I leaned back against the plush car seat and did the same. Around us, by the side of the road and into the forest, I cast out with my mind. I felt the heartbeats of a brood of young fox kits, frightened by the footstep of a doe nearby. I sensed a small field mouse and the silent swoop of an owl overhead, diving toward its prey in an elegant, deadly arc. I felt the quietness of the trees, their collective silence that had stood sentry and witness, rooted to that spot, in some cases, for over a century.

But there was no human presence in the woods.

A shudder rippled through Hunter, and I knew that he had felt what I had. Nothing.

"Was it—" Thinking again of Cal, I felt my body grow cold. "Do you think it was—a ghost?"

I didn't even know whether such a thing was possible, but Hunter didn't laugh at me. "I don't think so," he said slowly.

Something about his tone of voice made me ask, "Do you think it could be another message from your parents?"

For a moment Hunter was silent. "Yes," he said finally. "It

could be. But it could also have been a number of other things." I realized that Hunter was holding back, but I didn't ask him what he was thinking. I could guess. Amyranth. Ciaran.

"I think we should tell Erin about this," he said.

At the mention of her name, a mental image of Erin's appraising glance flashed through my mind and I felt a small pinprick of impatience. But I immediately pushed the feeling aside. Hunter was right, and I knew it. "When can we meet?" I asked.

"Are you free tomorrow night?" Hunter asked, and I nodded. That was the last thing we said as the car plodded forward at its snail's pace. Wrapped in fog, the night had a sense of unreality, and I was so, so glad to have Hunter sitting next to me—strong and sure, like the trees that loomed in the mist, standing guard over the forest.

The next day dawned clear and chilly, with a pale blue sky dotted with puffy clouds. Last fall's brown, brittle leaves danced by my windowpane on the breeze.

It was such a beautiful day, the incidents of the night before seemed unreal . . . and unlikely. Had everyone really freaked out over a few lightbulbs bursting? That could have been an electrical surge—a problem in the wiring at Hunter's house. And the figure in the fog could have just been an odd mist formation. Clouds took on strange shapes all the time, I reminded myself.

I lay in bed, enjoying the warmth of my flannel sheets and down comforter, listening for the sounds of my parents and sister as they went through their usual Sunday routine of showers and breakfasts. But the house was silent. Rolling over, I glanced at my digital clock. Nine forty-seven! They hadn't even bothered waking me for church.

I lay back against my pillows, unsure how I felt about that. Wicca was my religion, after all, the religion that felt like home to me, as natural as breathing. And I hadn't been going to church much lately. Still, our church filled me with warm feelings. It held lots of good memories for me, memories of my family and of my community.

Suddenly I felt like the last child to be picked up from a party—neglected and forgotten. I knew the feeling was childish, but I couldn't help it. It wasn't so much that I really wanted to go to church. I just wanted to be *asked*.

Slowly I crept out of bed, moving aside my cat, Dagda's, warm, furry form. He mewed softly, then stretched and rolled onto his back, only to curl up again and doze off. What a life.

After a long, steamy shower I began to feel almost human again. I puttered around the house awhile, reading the paper and microwaving myself a bowl of oatmeal. Desperate to talk to somebody, I called Robbie, but he wasn't home and I didn't leave a message. I didn't know what I wanted to say. Finally I decided to meet my parents for brunch at the Widow's Diner. It was a tradition for my family to eat there after church. This would be a good chance to show my mom that I could spend time with the family and still be involved in Wicca. Besides, I wanted to see them.

Quickly I pulled on a gray cable knit sweater and my faded jeans. I put on my thickest socks and sank my feet into my heavy brown boots. In just a few minutes I was in Das Boot, tearing up the road on the way to the Widow's Diner.

As I walked into the diner, my stomach squirmed with

nerves. Between Mary K being mad at me and the lecture I'd gotten from my mom, I wasn't sure what to expect. I glanced around and saw that my family was sitting in our usual spot—the booth against the windows. They were all laughing at something someone had said. Across from my mom and dad was the back of Mary K.'s head . . . and someone else, a girl with thick, golden brown hair. I stopped short. Who was that? Then my mom looked up and saw me. She looked surprised and pleased. She waved me over.

Mary K. turned around in her seat. After a moment she flashed me an uncertain smile, and the nervous caterpillars in my stomach quieted. Had she forgiven me? I hoped so. I grinned back and hurried toward them. The other girl still hadn't looked up, so I didn't see until I got to the table that it was Alisa.

"Hi, everyone," I said, sliding into the booth next to Mary K. The Formica tabletop was littered with my family's half-eaten lunch. "Hey, Alisa," I added when she didn't look up from the straw wrapper she was fiddling with on the table. For a moment I wondered what she was doing there. But I knew that she went to our church and that she and Mary K. had gotten pretty tight ever since Mary K.'s best friend, Jaycee, had found a boyfriend. Alisa had been close to Jaycee, too, so I guess that made both Alisa and Mary K. boyfriend refugees.

Alisa gave me a hesitant smile. "Hi," she said. There were dark circles under her eyes and a strange note in her voice that brought back the eerie scene from the night before. Instantly I remembered just how real it had all been. Alisa went back to fiddling with her straw wrapper.

"Have you eaten yet, sweetie?" my mom asked, and my dad twisted in his seat to flag the waitress down.

"Some oatmeal," I replied. "I really just came by to see you guys."

"Only oatmeal? Have a bagel," my mother urged, "or a cup of soup. It's lunchtime—you should have a bite to eat."

I realized that my parents wouldn't be satisfied until I ordered something, so I asked for some wheat toast and chamomile tea. By the time I'd finished ordering, my mom and dad were engrossed in a conversation about some problem she was having with her boss. I turned to say something to Mary K., but now she had her back to me. She was whispering something into Alisa's ear. My heart sank, and I had the strangest feeling. It was almost as if I were invisible. I sat quietly, staring out the window for a few moments, waiting for my tea. Here I was, right in the middle of my family—and missing them more than ever.

I spent the afternoon trying to do all the math homework that I should have done the week before. I actually finished most of it before I drove to Hunter and Sky's place at eight to meet with Erin.

Hunter let me in. Erin and Sky were sitting on the couch as we walked into the living room. The lamps were glowing with new lightbulbs, and the books sat quietly on their shelves. There was no sign of what had happened the night before.

"I've already told Sky and Erin about last night's fog," Hunter said as I pulled off my jacket and kicked off my duck boots. Padding across the room in my thick socks, I curled up into the corner of the large brown velvet armchair that sat to the side of the couch, pulling my legs beneath me.

"You say the shape you saw looked like a woman?" Erin said to Hunter. He nodded.

Erin pursed her lips. "Did she say anything?" she asked me abruptly.

I flushed slightly under her intense gaze. "No. She didn't do anything at all," I said. "She just looked at us a minute and disappeared."

Erin lifted her eyebrows and turned to Hunter for confirmation. He nodded again.

"But there's no doubt in your mind that this was *something*?" Erin asked. "This wasn't just some kind of problem with the weather—a strange-looking patch of mist?"

"It was real enough that I nearly drove the car off the road." Hunter's voice was certain, but I remembered the flash of doubt I'd felt that morning.

Erin sat back and pressed her lips together. She sat perfectly still, and with her pale skin and delicate features, she looked almost like she was made of marble.

"Do you think it was Ciaran?" Sky asked. Her oval face was tense.

"Perhaps," Erin said. Her gaze locked on my face.

The look made my stomach lurch. I felt afraid and defensive at the same time. "Do you think it was *me*?" I demanded.

Erin was unperturbed. "Perhaps," she replied coolly.

I opened my mouth to defend myself, but Erin cut me off. "Morgan, I merely said it was a possibility. You *may* be causing these incidents unconsciously—we simply can't rule it out. But right now, only two things are certain: strange things are happening, and they seem to involve you."

"Or Hunter," I pointed out.

"That's true," Hunter agreed. He quickly described what had happened in the movie theater a few nights before.

Erin seemed to ponder this a moment. "It seems that someone is trying to get in touch with one of you," she said. "Perhaps it's time we went looking for them."

"Should we scry?" Hunter asked.

"The sooner the better, I should think," Erin said. She disappeared into the kitchen for a moment and returned with a small stone bowl filled with water. I was intrigued by the fact that she chose to scry with water—I'd heard most witches found it unreliable.

We joined hands, and Erin began to chant as we gazed into the water. I'd never heard the words before, and they had an ancient quality that was both beautiful and terrifying. Although I didn't understand exactly what she was saying, I felt certain that Erin was calling on whoever was interfering with us to reveal him- or herself.

The water shimmered, and for a moment it almost seemed to glow silvery pink. The clock on the wall ticked on, but nothing happened. Erin began her low chant again, and this time Sky joined her. Still nothing.

Hunter sat to my left, and after a few moments I felt a shudder run through him. I squeezed his hand. I knew that he thought the strange incidents might have been messages for him from his parents. I knew that he was hoping they were— and that by scrying we would see them. I was struck with the irony of it—Hunter was hoping to see his father, while I was terrified to see my own. Hunter shuddered again. I turned to look at him just as a wave of pain and fear washed over me. It was flowing from him. He groaned and fell backward against the floor, as if he were being held there. Sweat broke out over his face, which had gone deadly white.

"Hunter!" I cried.

Erin leaned over Hunter and peered into his face as I brushed damp golden hair away from his forehead. Sky hurried behind him and put his head in her lap. Hunter moaned and began to say something. I didn't catch the beginning of it, but I heard him murmur something that sounded like, "Troptardeef." Then there was a string of words that made no sense to me.

I dug my fingernails into my palms. Goddess, please help him, I begged silently.

Hunter's body shuddered once more, then he lay still. His breathing was labored and ragged for a moment, then began to slow. Finally he opened his eyes. Looking up at me, he murmured, "What happened?"

I swallowed hard, unsure how to answer.

"Did you see anything?" Erin asked brusquely.

Hunter struggled to his elbows, and Sky helped him sit upright. He rubbed his head, then said, "Shadows. There was a narrow street, with cobblestones. And there was a wall. I . . . I was in a walled city."

"You said something," Erin informed him. "Do you remember what it was?"

Hunter shook his head. "No—I just remember the shadows . . . and the feelings. What did I say?"

"You said, 'It's too late—there's nothing I can do,'" Erin replied. "In French."

Hunter stared at her. "I don't speak French," he said.

Erin didn't reply to that. "Do you know why this happened?" she asked.

"No," Hunter replied. Then he said, "No," again, but his voice was less certain.

Erin leaned toward him. "Do you *think* you know why this happened?"

"I think it may have been one of my parents, trying to contact me," Hunter admitted.

"Hunter." Sky's voice was almost a gasp. "Are you sure?"

"No," he said quickly. "No, I'm not. That's only what I think it was. But it could be anything."

The words settled over me like a cold weight, sinking into my bones. A feeling came over me—it was the same feeling I'd had the night before, when Hunter and I had rounded the bend in the road. It was a deep feeling of dread.

I reached for Hunter's hand and felt slightly better at the familiar warmth of his touch. I was worried for him. But more than that, I was worried about the future. Worried about us. I didn't know what the messages meant . . . but I had a horrible feeling that their power was great enough to tear us apart.

"Morgan, I think we had better begin our lessons as soon as possible," Erin said. "Are you free tomorrow afternoon?"

"Yes, of course. Where should we meet?" I asked. "Here?"

"Actually," Hunter broke in, "Alyce suggested that you hold your lessons in the back room of Practical Magick. She thought it might be a good idea in case you need any books or tools."

I nodded. "That works for me."

"For me as well," Erin said.

Everyone was subdued as we said good night. Sky seemed particularly pensive. As I laced up my heavy boots and pulled on my jacket, I wondered what she was thinking.

"That was frustrating," I said as Hunter walked me to Das Boot.

"I know," he agreed. "I just wish we knew what all of this meant."

I remembered the violence of exploding lightbulbs and kamikaze books. Could Hunter's parents really have been behind those things? It seemed unlikely. I thought of my own father—Ciaran. That sort of violence was more his style.

As if he'd been reading my mind, Hunter said, "Morgan, I heard from Eoife this afternoon. The council has found out Ciaran is definitely in Spain. They're closing in. It's only a matter of time before they have him in custody. Eoife said to tell you they couldn't have done it without you."

Relief swept over me, followed by anger, startling me with its strength. Anger at the council for making me spy on my own father. Anger at Ciaran for all the evil he had done, for the taint he had passed on to me. Anger at myself for the tug of kinship I still felt for him. "Oh, no problem. I'm great at spying on my relatives," I said bitterly. "Just let me know if you need any info on Mary K."

"He's dangerous," Hunter said quietly. "You did right, even though it was hard."

I closed my eyes and tried to let Hunter's voice calm me. I knew my father was dangerous. But when I was with Ciaran, I'd felt a strange connection—something I'd never felt before. Knowing that this man was my real father, that his blood ran in my veins, had given me a visceral sense of belonging. I felt that I knew Ciaran almost better than I knew the members of my adopted family because part of him was in me.

And I knew his true name.

The thought echoed up from the depths of my mind. I

knew Ciaran's true name. He'd said it in a forbidden spell he'd used when he was trying to win me to his side.

When you know someone's true name, you can control him.

I had never told Hunter. I could have told him right then. I could have said Ciaran's true name. But I didn't. They already have the sigil, I told myself. Hunter's right; they're going to capture him soon. They don't need his true name.

"If Ciaran is the one sending these messages," Hunter said fiercely, "he will be very, very sorry." His words slashed through the chill air like a blade.

"Do you wish you were there—in Spain, tracking him?" I asked. I had seen Hunter put the braigh on Cal once, and once on David Redstone. The spelled silver chain burned witches' skin, raising angry red blisters. I knew that Hunter hadn't enjoyed using it either time. But now I wondered how he would feel putting it on the wrists of the man who'd almost killed both of us more than once.

"My job is to protect you," Hunter said simply. "According to the council, that is my sole responsibility for the moment."

I frowned. "That doesn't answer my question."

"Doesn't it?"

Hunter gazed at the hulking forms of the trees, and I suddenly realized the full weight of what he was saying. He thought he was receiving messages from his parents. And he couldn't do anything about it because he had to stay in Widow's Vale to take care of me. That had to be incredibly frustrating. More. It had to be agonizing.

"Can't you tell the council how important this is to you?" I asked. "If they catch Ciaran, I won't be in danger anymore."

Hunter shook his head, not looking at me. "The council wants me here."

I looked at him, feeling a rush of sympathy. I thought of how very young Hunter had been when his parents had disappeared. I could only imagine how fiercely he wanted them back. "I'm sorry," I whispered.

Hunter didn't speak. He just reached out, took my hand, and brought it briefly to his lips before letting it go.

"I'll help you find them," I said.

"Good," was the last thing he said before retreating up his front walk. He didn't look back as I got in my car and drove away.

5.
Forces

Morgan lost it last night. I don't know if she went crazy or if her powers short-circuited or something, but things started flying around the room and exploding, and it scared the holy crap out of me.

Now I don't know what to do. The circle started off really well. I don't know much about Wicca, but there's something about it that feels almost like a tune I only half remember from childhood. The words are long forgotten, but if I try hard enough, I'll remember the melody, and everything will fall into place.

That was the way I felt last night . . . for a while.

Morgan's magick feels like something else. I'm afraid of it in the way I used to be afraid of leaving my closet door open when I was five years old.

I wish she'd just leave the coven. Then Mary K would feel better and I wouldn't have to be afraid anymore.

—Alisa

Mr. Powell waited until the last five minutes of class to pass back the graded exams.

The class buzzed as he made his way around the room, placing papers facedown on desks. "Well done," he whispered to Claire Kennedy, and, "Great job," to Andy Nasewell. Hope fluttered in my chest. Andy wasn't a great student. Maybe I hadn't done as badly as I thought.

Mr. Powell slapped a paper on my desk. His hand was still a moment as he looked down at me. "See me after class," he said. Crap. I turned the paper over, my heart thumping. At the top there was a big red number. Sixty-three.

The bell rang and everyone streamed out of the classroom, comparing papers and chatting. Quickly I shoved my exam inside my binder and shuffled up to Mr. Powell's desk. I could hardly even look at him.

"Morgan," he said, folding his arms on his desk, "we've spoken about this before. Your grade in this class has dropped significantly since first semester, and I'd hoped to see more improvement." Mr. Powell looked up at me. He was a good teacher—the kind who really seemed to care about his students—and he looked concerned.

"I know I messed up," I replied. "I've just been a little . . . overwhelmed lately."

"This was the second of four major exams for this marking period," Mr. Powell said. "The exams are what determine your final grade."

I did a quick mental calculation. Even if I got a hundred on each of the other two exams, my final average would be a seventy-eight. *Seventy-eight.* That was pretty far from my usual honor roll standards.

"You do realize, Morgan, that junior-year grades are what most colleges look at when they are determining admissions," Mr. Powell went on. "I'm afraid I'm going to have to let your parents know about this."

Oh, no. "Is there anything I can do?" I asked. "Some extra credit or something?"

Mr. Powell thought for a moment. "I don't like to give one person a shot at extra credit without giving the whole class the same chance," he said slowly.

"I'm sure other people would like to bring up their grades," I suggested.

Mr. Powell sighed. "All right," he said. "I'll announce it to the class tomorrow. Write a five- to eight-page paper on any historical subject for a maximum of twenty extra points on the next exam."

I stifled a groan. Twenty points. That didn't sound like much. But when I did the average in my head along with two other perfect exams, I realized I could end up with an eighty-three average for the marking period—a B. It would be tough, but I could do it. "Thanks, Mr. Powell," I said quickly, and turned toward the door.

"Morgan," he called after me.

"Yes?" I paused in the doorway.

He looked at me over the tops of his bifocals. "Make it good," he said.

"Did you talk to Robbie?" I asked Bree as we walked out of English. It was our last class. I hadn't seen her or Robbie all day, except from a distance—neither one of them was at the usual spot in the morning or at lunch, either.

Bree hugged her notebooks to her chest. "No," she admitted. She was wearing a long black leather skirt and a woolly black sweater with a plunging neckline, and it made her look mysterious and a little sad.

I wasn't all that surprised. Bree hated "relationship" talks. "Why not?"

"To be honest, Robbie was pretty freaked out by the circle on Saturday," Bree said. "Yesterday didn't really seem like the best time for a chat, you know?"

"Bree, you need to talk to him," I said.

"I know, I know." Bree hesitated, her dark eyes clouding over. "Actually," she said finally, "I think maybe *you* should talk to Robbie. That scene at the circle scared the crap out of him. God, Morgan, it scared the crap out of everyone. Me too."

"But that wasn't *me*," I insisted. "It scared me, too."

We stood there in the hall for a moment, just staring at each other as students streamed past us. I had no idea what to say. Finally Bree reached out and grabbed my hand. "Look, Morgan. If you say it wasn't you, then I believe it. I'll talk to Robbie for you. But you should know that he's worried about you and so am I." To my dismay, her eyes filled with tears. Bree wasn't a big weeper. "We're friends, right?"

I swallowed hard. "Right."

"Okay." Bree gave me a watery smile. "I'll talk to him. About both things."

She dropped my hand and turned toward her locker. I trudged to mine, silently cursing these strange things that kept happening. I was as afraid of them as everyone else. Yet everyone thought I was behind them.

Standing in front of my locker, I felt a faint, icy breeze blow past me. The small hairs at the back of my neck rose. Had anyone else felt it? To my right, I saw Cindy Halpern struggling with her locker combination. Maybe it was just my imagination.

I spun the lock and yanked on my locker door. It swung open with a bang. I jumped back to avoid the avalanche of books and papers that cascaded out.

"God, Morgan," Cindy said, rolling her eyes at the mess, "get a Trapper Keeper."

I ignored her. My instincts were clamoring. It was true that my locker was a royal disaster, but the way my stuff had shot out of it. . . . I peered down the hall to see if other strange things were happening, but all I saw was students shoving books into backpacks and pulling on jackets. I cast my senses, but I didn't sense any sort of sinister presence. Frowning, I eyed the mess on the floor. Maybe it really was just the result of a locker that hadn't been cleaned out in a while. I bent and started gathering papers.

"Need some help?" asked a voice behind me.

I glanced up as Alisa crouched and began stacking my books. "This looks like the bottom of my dad's closet," she said. Her voice was heavy, and she seemed tired.

I stopped gathering my papers and looked at her. "Are you okay?" I asked.

Alisa frowned. "Actually, no," she said. "I—I wanted to tell you. . . . I'm leaving the coven."

I was so surprised, I sat down on the floor. "You are?" I asked. The image of Bree with tears in her eyes, telling me that Robbie was worried about me, clicked into my brain. "Why?" I asked carefully.

Alisa ran her fingers through her hair, pulling it away

from her oval face. "Things are just going too far for me."
She looked down at the floor, then up at me. "The magick
I've seen lately . . . it scares me. These are powerful forces,
Morgan." She leaned toward me until I could see myself
reflected in her eyes. "They're dangerous."

I got the feeling that Alisa wanted me to promise that
nothing frightening would happen at a circle again. But I
couldn't. I didn't have any idea what had caused the strange
magick on Saturday—and I certainly didn't have any control
over it. "I'm sorry, Alisa," I said finally. "I guess you have to
do what's right for you."

Alisa looked at me a moment and then nodded. "Okay.
But I just wanted to tell you . . . I have a bad feeling. The
magick you've been practicing is bad for everyone. I'm talking about the whole coven," she said in a low voice. "I think
you should stop what you're doing. Be careful, Morgan."

"Yeah, Morgan, be careful," said a voice above us. It was
Mary K., her book bag slung over one shoulder. I tried to read
the expression on my sister's face. Mary K. and I hadn't had a
real conversation since the night of Hunter's dinner, but I'd felt
that she was softening toward me a bit—and now she was obviously here so I would give her a ride home. I hoped she hadn't
overheard anything just now that would freak her out again.

"What does Morgan have to be careful about?" Mary K.
asked Alisa.

I waited nervously. Alisa glanced at me, then picked up a
pile of my books. "She has to be careful not to get buried in
this pile of crap," Alisa said as she slid my books into place
on the shelf. "I was just recommending that Morgan wear
bright-colored clothing so we can find her if she gets hidden

in the next locker paperslide."

I gathered the rest of my papers and scrambled to my feet. "Just a second, Mary K.," I said. "Let me find what I need. I'll be ready to roll in a minute."

"Actually," Mary K. said, "I'm here for Alisa. We're going over to her house to study." She turned to Alisa. "Ready?"

"Sure," Alisa replied. "See you around, Morgan," she said over her shoulder as she turned to walk down the hall.

"See you later," Mary K. added, giving me a small wave. "I called Mom already—I won't be home for dinner." She trotted after Alisa.

"Okay," I said. "See you." Watching their retreating figures, I couldn't help feeling a little stab of jealousy . . . and fear. Sure, Alisa had just covered for me now—but what if later she told Mary K. that the coven was dealing with powerful forces? What if she described what had happened on Saturday night?

Would my sister turn against me even more?

6.
Restricted

I tried to talk to Morgan today. I told her that I was uncomfortable with some of the magick being used in Kithic. So, naturally, Morgan said, "Oh, Alisa, thank you so much for telling me. I'm sure that if you're uneasy, others in the coven must be, too. I'll be sure to tone down my freakish witch powers so that we can all enjoy the simple, quiet magick of Wicca together without unleashing dark forces of the underworld over which we have no control."

Yeah, right. Actually, what she said was more like, "Whatever. Too bad for you."

So now I've said that I'm leaving Kithic. There's only one problem. That means I actually have to <u>leave</u> Kithic. There's a nursery rhyme that keeps repeating in my mind. I think my mom must have said it to me when I was little: "No beginning or end to hearth, home, or friend." It's about belonging.

I feel like I belong in Kithic. But Morgan doesn't care.

I wonder if The other people in Kithic have really Thought about what Morgan is doing. I mean, her powers _are_ amazing. I guess it's possible That everyone is so wrapped up in The mystique That They haven't really bothered To Think about what she's doing or where it might lead. Or maybe They have, but They just cover up better Than I do.

It's not That I Think Morgan is evil. I just don't Think she realizes how dangerous she is. Maybe I should write a letter To The Town paper To warn people That This is happening. It feels kind of underhanded. But This is dangerous stuff. I feel That people have a right To know.

I just don't want anyone To get hurt.

—Alisa

The bell over the door at Practical Magick jingled as I walked inside. Closing the door quickly against the cold, I breathed in the warm spicy scent of incense and the familiar smell of old books. Alyce looked up at me from behind the counter, and her face instantly broke into a smile. "Morgan," she said. "You've got a visitor."

There were two other people in the store, browsing through the herbs. "Is she here already?" I whispered as I walked to the counter.

Alyce nodded gravely. "In the back."

I grimaced. That meant I was late. "Thanks." I hurried past the tall wooden bookshelves toward the curtain that separated the rear of the store. I was irked that I couldn't stop to chat with Alyce. Besides being the owner of Practical Magick, she was the leader of the Starlocket coven and a good friend. We'd been through a lot together these last few months.

"You're late," Erin said coolly as I pulled back the curtain and stepped into the combination storeroom-office.

"So I heard," I replied, sliding into the folding chair across from hers. I hadn't gotten much sleep the night before and wasn't in the best of moods.

Erin's eyes flashed. "Morgan, I am here at the behest of the council. I've traveled a long way to get here," she said. "And I've got less than two weeks to teach you everything I know about magickal defenses."

"Sorry," I mumbled to the table. Okay, so I was late. Was that the world's biggest tragedy? Did she have to treat me like a five-year-old? It was bad enough that the reason I was late was that my English teacher had grabbed me on my way out of school and lectured me for twenty minutes about how I wasn't "working up to potential."

Erin leaned forward, and I felt compelled to look up at her. "There are some members of the council who put a great deal of stock in your powers," she said in a voice that sounded almost like a purr or a growl. "But let me tell you something—those powers will never be anything but a dangerous toy until you learn to control them."

There was half a moment while we stared at each other and I felt Erin's intensity like heat from a fire.

"Here we are!" said a voice. Suddenly the curtain was pulled back and Alyce bustled in with a teapot and mugs. She glanced at Erin. "Licorice still your favorite?"

I looked from one to the other. "Do you two know each other already?" I asked.

"Of course," Alyce said. "We've been friends for years."

I tried to hide my surprise. They were friends? But they were such opposites—Erin seemed as hard as steel, while Alyce was about as hard as a feather bed.

"We haven't seen each other in a long time, though," Erin said, smiling at Alyce.

"Too long," Alyce said. "Which reminds me. I've been saving something for you." Pulling a key ring out of her pocket, she crossed to a heavy wooden desk at the back of the room. She opened one of the drawers and pulled out a large gray metal box. Then she chose another key, opened the box, and pulled out something large and flat and wrapped in a piece of dark cloth. When she came closer, I saw that it was a square of black silk. My pulse quickened. Black silk had strong blocking properties—it was often used to wrap magickal objects that might be dangerous. Alyce put the object on the table, then pulled the fabric away from it, revealing an ancient leather-bound book.

"Where did you get this?" Erin whispered. She'd gone pale.

"At a library sale, if you can believe it," Alyce said. "About a year ago. I don't think they had any idea what they were selling."

I read the faded gold lettering on the cover. *On the Containement of Magick,* it said. "Harris Stoughton," I said aloud, looking at the author's name. It sounded vaguely familiar to me.

"A horrible man," Erin said. "A witch who used hysteria to wipe out other witches."

When she said that, I remembered where I'd heard the name before—from some of my reading on the Salem witch trials. I hadn't read anything about him being a witch, though.

"I thought that you should have it," Alyce said to Erin. "I

don't like keeping it here, but I don't want it to fall into the wrong hands, either."

Erin flipped through a few of the pages warily, as if the book were something dangerous, then snapped the cover closed. "It's a rare book." Looking up at Alyce, she added, "Thank you. A book like this can be dangerous, but it can also be useful." Erin faced me. "The first rule of magickal defenses is 'Know your enemy.'"

The bell over the front door jingled, and Alyce went to see to the customers.

Erin pushed herself up from the table and walked over to the curtain. Tracing her fingers around its edges, she muttered a harsh-sounding phrase. "Now no one will be able to hear us," she explained when she saw my confused expression. "Ready?"

I stood up and followed her to the center of the room. We faced each other for a moment. In a flash Erin caught my wrist, and I felt a crackle of electricity ripple through me. But I had been expecting this move. Quickly I threw up a block, as Hunter had taught me. Instead of building, the energy quickly dissipated through my body. Where she held my wrist, I felt the energy die in Erin's hand as well.

Erin stepped back. "That was good," she said simply. "You know the divagnth. And you're strong."

Damn straight, I thought, feeling a rush of pride.

Erin took a step away from me. I took in her small form. I stood at least a full head taller than her. I felt great— strangely strong, physically powerful, as if I'd been pumping iron or something. Weird, I thought. But very cool.

"Things are not always as they appear," Erin said. As I

stood wondering what that meant, she suddenly seemed to grow taller. Her mouth elongated, and she smiled, revealing long sharp fangs, each as thick as my finger. I felt my pride evaporate as her shoulders broadened and her green eyes turned darker, glowing with a cruel light.

I shrank away from her as cold panic washed over me like a slap of icy water. With horror, I understood that she was more powerful than I was and that she was evil. Why hadn't I seen it before? She had put up a spell so that no one could hear us, and now she was going to kill me and take my magick.

Erin—or whatever the thing before me truly was—sent out slim wisps of gray smoke. The dark vapor grew thicker and began to fill the room. I felt myself choking.

The creature took a step toward me, and I stumbled away from it. It opened its horrible jaws. "Fight," it said in a voice that was more animal than human. "Fight me."

I racked my brain for a blocking spell, but I couldn't think clearly. My body was pulsing with adrenaline. Did Alyce know that Erin was evil? Did Hunter know? What would happen to them once I was gone and this thing had my magick? I had survived so much in the last few months. Was this really how I would be done in?

The creature leaned toward me as the darkness closed in. I didn't know what to do. Blindly I threw out my hands and sent a white ball of energy at the creature. It was fearsome-looking, brilliant and powerful. I had never called up something like that before, and for a moment I felt a surge of hope. But the creature merely made a flicking gesture with its left arm and deflected the ball across the room. It slammed against a metal shelving unit with an enormous crash. Back stock of notebooks flew off the top shelf and rained all over the floor. I could hardly see anything through the black vapor. I cowered against the wall behind me and finally sank to the floor.

The creature reached out a claw and grabbed my shoulder. "Morgan," said a voice through the darkness. It was a lovely, musical voice, and for a moment I couldn't remember where I'd heard it before. "Morgan," it repeated, "are you all right?"

I looked down at the horrifying claw on my shoulder. Slowly it began to shift and change. The thick, muddy gray skin began to lighten, and the cruel claws receded until it was nothing but a small, pale hand almost the size of a child's. I looked up into Erin's clear green gaze. "Are you all right?" she repeated.

The fog around me began to lift, and I sat up. "What happened?"

"Take a deep breath," Erin advised. "Now release it. Do it again," she urged. "Focus on the breath. Now ground yourself."

Leaning forward, I placed my forehead against the cool tile floor. Slowly my head cleared. "You need to learn to control your emotions," Erin said. "Pride and fear can cut you off from your power and leave you vulnerable. I'm sorry," she added as I sat up. "You fooled me with the divagnth. I didn't realize you weren't ready for that lesson."

Standing up, Erin reached out her hand and pulled me to my feet. "You're strong, Morgan," she said. "That's your weakness."

I frowned. "That doesn't make sense."

"You have strong native power," Erin explained. "Strong abilities. You just called up white witch fire, no easy task. But you don't have control." She gestured toward the scorched metal shelves and the Books of Shadows that had spilled all over the floor. "That makes you dangerous."

"But you're here to teach me control," I protested.

"Morgan," she said with forced patience, "I understand that you've been in a complicated situation. I don't know all the details, but I do know that you've been forced into a situation in which you've had to begin your education in the middle of things, instead of at the proper beginning."

"What are you saying?" I asked warily.

"I'm saying that you should back up." Erin's voice was brittle. "Take a break from magick that is too advanced for you and focus instead on learning your plants and witch history. I know it's not what you want to hear, but when you're sailing in the wrong direction, sometimes it's faster to go back than it is to keep pushing on until you've gone around the world."

"I feel like you're punishing me," I said bitterly.

"It's for your own safety." Erin's voice was like a door slamming shut, and I knew that there was no use arguing. "And it's not forever, Morgan," she added. "We'll begin again tomorrow, at the library. At three-thirty sharp."

The bell over the door jingled again—the customers leaving—and Alyce poked her head through the curtain. "Is everything okay back here?" she asked. Her eyes fell on the ruined mass of notebooks. "Oh, my."

"We were just about to clean that up," I said quickly. Erin and I walked over to the pile of Books of Shadows and began brushing them off and placing them back on the shelf. Thankfully, most of them were undamaged. Erin told Alyce that she would pay for the ones that were.

"It's my fault," Erin told her, digging in her bag. "Besides, the cost of a few blank Books of Shadows isn't one-tenth of the value of this book." She jerked her head in the direction of *On the Containement of Magick*.

I watched Erin hug Alyce as we said good-bye. Erin was stiff, but her affection seemed real as she tucked the silk-wrapped book under her arm. Then again, she'd seemed pretty real when she'd looked like a hideous monster only half an hour before.

I sensed who was calling a second before the phone rang.

"I'll get it," I called, starting up from the dining-room table, where I was doing my homework. But it was already too late.

"Hello?" my mom's voice said from the kitchen. Dad was working late, so she and I were the only ones home. We'd finished dinner about two hours ago, and Mom had been working on her various documents in the kitchen since then.

"Yes, this is she," I heard her say. "Oh, hello. Yes. What? Well—no, she didn't. I see. Mmm-hmm." Even through the door, I could hear the edge of anger dawning in my mom's voice.

I stared down at the books and notebooks spread out before me and tried to focus on the analysis of vectors I was doing for physics, but it was no use.

"Was that out of a hundred points?" I heard my mother ask, and I bit my lip.

After a moment I heard Mom hang up, and the door between the dining room and the kitchen swung open. "Morgan, we need to talk." Her voice was grim.

My stomach churned. I put down my pencil. "Okay."

Sitting down across from me, my mom said, "I just got a phone call from your history teacher, Mr. Powell."

I didn't even bother trying to act surprised. "I know," I said.

"He's concerned about your grade in his class. So am I."

"I know," I said again. Shifting in my seat, I added, "I've already talked to him about doing some extra credit—"

Holding up her hand traffic-cop style, my mom cut me off. "Morgan, I'm not happy about the fact that you failed two tests. But I'm even more unhappy about the fact that you hid it from Dad and me. When were you going to tell us?"

"I thought that if I brought my grade up—"

"But what if you didn't?" my mom interrupted. "Mr. Powell says that these two exams count for fifty percent of your final grade. Were you going to wait until you failed the class to let us know that there was a problem?" She ran her fingers through her russet hair in an I-don't-know-what-to-do-with-you gesture.

"With extra credit, I could still get a B in the class!"

"You could still get an F!" my mom snapped. "Have you even started this extra-credit work?"

I dug through my stack of papers and pulled out the notes I'd already made for my history paper. I didn't realize until after I'd handed them to my mom that I was making a horrible mistake.

"This can't be your history paper." Mom's voice was tense. "What *is* this?"

"We're allowed to write on any subject," I explained weakly.

She simply looked at me for a moment, then slapped the notes down on the table in frustration. "Why do you have to test us? You *know* how Dad and I feel about witchcraft nonsense!"

"The Salem witch trials aren't nonsense," I pointed out, my own temper starting to flare. "They were an important historical event."

"That's not the point. Morgan, your interest in Wicca has grown to the point where it's crowding out almost everything else," my mom said. "I don't want you throwing your future away."

"I'm not!" I cried. "How can you say that?"

"Look," my mother went on. "I don't want to fight about the witch stuff right now. Your grades have to improve, and I don't see that happening. This is your final warning. If those grades don't improve, Dad and I are going to start talking seriously about changing your environment."

What? This had never come up before. "What do you mean?"

"Saint Anne's has a few openings," my mother said. "It's a very good school."

My jaw dropped open. "It's a Catholic school." My voice was harsh. "You'd really send me to a Catholic school?"

"Why not? The average class size is fourteen students, so they would be able to give you a lot of individual attention." She reached out and touched my hair almost pleadingly. "We want to help you, Morgan."

I stared at her. As if yanking me away from all my friends and sticking me into a place where they still believed in corporal punishment would help! The words *I'm not Catholic* sprang to my lips, but I couldn't bring myself to say them. It seemed almost like a declaration of war. It wasn't exactly true, anyway. Catholicism was the religion I was raised with, and I still felt like I *was* a Catholic in many ways. "Please, Mom," I answered instead. "Don't do that. I'll—I'll go to the library every day. I'll bring my grades up, I swear."

"We'll see." My mom pushed my history notes across

the table at me and stood up. "Family night is tomorrow," she said wearily. "At six."

"I'll be there." My voice sounded hollow.

She trudged out of the room. I watched her go, then looked down at my books.

I had a lot of work to do.

"I just don't think I can study with Erin right now," I said to Hunter. I was using the phone in the kitchen, summarizing the conversation I'd had with my mom earlier that evening. My parents and Mary K. had gone to bed, but I—the night owl—would be up for another few hours. "I just can't, can't get sent to Catholic school."

"That would be awful," Hunter agreed quietly.

"But my grades are really in the gutter."

Hunter sighed. "Isn't there any way that you can learn from Erin and still improve your grades?" he asked. "We can try to make sure you have time to finish your schoolwork, too. It's very important that you study with Erin right now. Especially with all the mysterious things that have been happening."

Pushing aside some of my mom's paperwork detritus, I made room for the cup of tea I'd just brewed. I took a sip, debating whether or not to tell Hunter what had happened with Erin earlier that day. "Actually, Erin doesn't even want to teach me magick," I admitted finally. "She just wants me to study witch history and plants."

"Those things are important, too," Hunter replied.

I stared at the receiver a minute, unable to believe he was taking her side. How typical. "Oh, yeah, they'll come in real handy if I'm ever attacked by the dark forces," I said sarcastically.

"I'm here to protect you in case that happens," Hunter reminded me. "And basic knowledge is necessary to learn more advanced magick. Witch history, herbs, runes—all of these things are part of the initiation rites. Erin is right to make sure you know them. Once you're a full apprentice, then you can start learning more magick and more spells. You know more than most initiates already."

I sighed. "It's just hard to see the value in that. I mean, you know the dangers of the dark forces even better than I do. I need to learn about them."

"I know." Hunter's voice was gentle. "But you have to look at the big picture. The sooner you can be initiated as a blood witch, the better. Once you're in total control of your powers, Morgan, you'll be a great asset."

I rolled my eyes. Sometimes Hunter had a real gift for making things sound unromantic. "All right," I said. "I'll figure out a way to do both." We said our good-byes, and I stood up to place the phone in its cradle. When I turned around, I nearly jumped a foot in the air. "God, Mary K.," I said, placing my palm on my chest. "You scared me."

She stood in the doorway in a white nightgown. Beneath the fluorescent kitchen lights, she looked pale and strange.

"What's wrong?" I asked quickly.

"Alisa was right," she said in a low voice.

I swallowed hard, mentally running through the conversation I'd just had with Hunter. How much of it had she overheard? "What are you talking about?" I stalled.

"You *know* what I'm talking about." Mary K.'s whisper had the intensity of a scream. "My God, Morgan—don't try to cover this up with *lies*."

I jammed my hands into the soft pockets of my flannel robe. "Look, Mary K., I don't know what you heard—"

"I want you to leave the coven." The words hung there, ugly and irrefutable, as Mary K. folded her arms across her chest.

"No." I shook my head. "I'm sorry, but—"

"Morgan, don't you get it?" Mary K. interrupted. "This isn't just about you. What about Mom and Dad? They don't have any idea what's really going on! How do you think they'll feel if anything happens to you?" Her voice wavered, and she tucked a strand of hair behind her ear. "How do you think *I'll* feel if something happens . . . and I never even warned them?"

I stood there wordlessly for a long time. I understood what she was saying . . . but what could I do about it? I couldn't leave the coven now. I had chosen Wicca, and it had chosen me. And even though I wanted to comfort Mary K., I knew I couldn't lie to her. In the end, I just said, "I'm sorry."

Mary K. was still standing in the kitchen when I went up to my room. I lay in my bed, listening for her footsteps, on the stairs for a long, long time. She still hadn't come upstairs by the time I finally fell asleep.

7.
Danger

September 22, 1971

Today was Andrew Lewis's funeral. Mother and Father didn't want us to go, but Sam insisted, and in the end our parents had to give in. I don't often have a chance to go to a Catholic church for any reason, and I was surprised at how much I enjoyed the service. Sunlight streamed in the stained glass windows, and the whole ceremony seemed very ancient and peaceful, even though it was a bit too solemn. I couldn't help comparing it with the circle we'd held the night before at Patience Stamp's house. She's a potter, and her house is very simple but filled with beautiful handmade things. We'd held hands and had felt the magick flow between us, easing the pain we felt at losing our friends to the sea. I felt the same kind of magick in the church—a healing magick that exists between people. In the middle of the service I noticed that tears were streaming down Sam's cheeks, and I handed him a tissue. I was touched by his sorrow. But later I discovered he was feeling more than simple sorrow.

After the service Sam walked into my room and sat on the edge of my bed. When I saw that he was holding The Book—the Harris Stoughton book—I was afraid.

Then Sam told me that he'd tried a small spell— a weather spell—because it hadn't rained for so long. He'd just wanted to see if he could call up a little rain, so about ten days ago, when the moon was waxing, he'd tried it. He hadn't known what would happen, he said, so it couldn't really be his fault, could it?

It took about half a minute for this to sink in. When I realized what he was telling me, I could hardly breathe. How could he? How? The storm that killed the crew of the <u>Lady Marie</u> was his fault. I grabbed him by the collar and started to shake him. <u>"What have you done?"</u> I was almost screaming, and Sam started bawling. The Book fell from his lap, and I dove for it. It felt warm in my hand, like something alive, and I wanted to throw it down, but I didn't dare.

I must burn the vile thing before it destroys us all.
—Sarah Curtis

"Morgan!" I knew the voice was Bree's, but I couldn't reply or even turn my head because I was gripping a paper cup of tea in my teeth as my cold fingers fumbled to lock the door of my car. Plumes of steam rose from the hot liquid and combined with my breath, dissipating quickly.

"Here," Bree said as she reached for the paper cup.

I released it gratefully. "Thanks."

"Got a minute?" Bree asked.

"Sure," I said taking the tea back from her. "What's up?"

"Robbie and I broke up."

I choked on the sip of tea I'd just taken. "What?" I looked at Bree more closely. Her face was ashen, and her eyes were red-rimmed. She wasn't kidding.

Bree glanced at my car. "Can we——?"

"Of course." I put my tea on the roof of the car and unlocked the door. A quick glance at my watch told me that we had ten minutes until the first bell. "What do you mean, you broke up? What happened?" I asked when we were seated inside the car.

"Just what I said. Robbie and I talked last night." Bree gave a small half shrug, lifting only one shoulder. "He said he needed space."

I waited a moment. "And——?" I prompted.

"That's it." Bree gazed straight ahead. The parking lot was filling up as teachers and students hurried to class.

"Bree," I said, "that doesn't necessarily mean that Robbie wants to break up." I didn't *think* it did, anyway. If it did, I was going to have to have a long talk with Robbie.

Bree flashed me an oh-grow-up glance. "Spare me. I know what it means." Raking her fingers through her hair, she added, "Not that it really matters, anyway. I mean, the relationship was getting a little old. I've been thinking about dating other people."

"Bree," I said gently, "it's me. Don't."

She turned toward me and her facade broke. Her eyes welled up, tears ran down her cheeks, and she looked like the same Bree whose heart was broken by Todd Hall in the seventh grade. "I know. I just—I just needed to say something bitchy."

I opened my mouth. But just then the first-period bell sounded, far away, and Bree opened the car door and stepped out.

"Bree," I called after her, "talk to Robbie!" But she'd already slammed the door and was striding toward the school. I didn't know whether she'd heard me, and I wasn't even sure that it mattered.

"I should be home by six," I said into a pay phone in the lobby of the public library later that day.

"Great," my mom said at the other end of the line. "I was thinking for family night we could play some board games and make hot fudge sundaes."

Even the faint crackle of static on the line couldn't disguise my mom's excitement. I got the feeling that she was trying to make peace after our argument the night before. "Sounds great, Mom," I said, suddenly struck with a pang of guilt. I'd told my mom that I was at the library to study history and science—but I hadn't mentioned it was witch history and magickal botany with Erin. And here she was, planning fun activities for the whole family. I was a terrible daughter. "See you at six."

I hung up, feeling lousy.

"Everything all right?" Erin asked as I plopped down across from her.

I laced my fingers together and rested my chin on them. "Just parental stuff."

Erin peered at me. As usual with her, I felt like I needed to explain myself. "It's just—they're Catholics. They don't approve of witchcraft. And they're threatening to send me to Catholic school."

Erin nodded gravely. "I wonder what your mother would think of all this."

For a moment I was confused—hadn't we just been talking about my mother? Then I realized that Erin was talking about Maeve, my birth mother. My heart suddenly skipped a beat.

I had never known my birth mother. She was from Ireland and had only come to America with her lover, Angus, after their entire coven was decimated by the dark wave. Coming to America hadn't saved her, though. Ciaran—her other, secret lover—caught up with her and killed her while I was still a baby.

"Did you know her?" I asked Erin. My throat was suddenly dry.

"I met her once, briefly, when she was about fifteen and I was twenty-one," Erin said. "My dearest friend, Mary, married a Belwicket man." Her eyes clouded.

Belwicket was the name of Maeve's coven. "Your friend—did she—"

"Gone," Erin said. "Like everyone else."

We sat together in silence for a moment.

"I can't imagine what it must have been like for you, growing up in a house without magick," she said. Her eyebrows were raised, and her face held a question.

"It wasn't a big deal," I admitted. "I never knew anything else." I paused. The next part was harder to talk about.

"Until I met Cal." I looked at Erin, unsure how much of the story she already knew.

Erin nodded. "Sgàth," she said, using Cal's witch name. The word sounded like a low susurration, the voice of the wind in the trees. She knew who he was. Of course.

"Yes. He taught me about Wicca, and I started learning more on my own. I discovered that I had powers. And then I learned the truth. That my parents weren't my birth parents . . . and that I was Woodbane."

"Morgan," Erin said, leaning toward me. "You haven't had an easy time of it. But that just means you have to be willing to work very hard—harder than most others have to. Are you willing to do that?"

I didn't hesitate. "Yes," I said.

"Good." Erin held up a small slip of paper. "I've checked the computer. The library has a number of fascinating books on witch history. We can start there." She handed the paper to me. On it was a list of five books and their call numbers.

"I'll be right back," I said. As I headed over to the nonfiction section of the library, I passed a familiar auburn head bent over a notebook at a nearby table. Mary K. She had gotten a ride with Susan Wallace both before and after school—clearly avoiding me again. Alisa sat across from her, murmuring in a low voice. Whispering in my sister's ear about my evil powers, no doubt.

A voice in my mind urged me to go and find the books. I knew it was the smart thing to do, but I just couldn't make myself do it. There was something about the way Alisa looked, sitting there—I wanted to get her away from Mary K. Things were tense enough with my family. I didn't want

Alisa getting into the middle of it. I crossed the room in a few quick strides and stood next to my sister. "Hey, you guys," I whispered, trying to sound as nonchalant as possible.

Mary K. looked up with a start and placed her hand casually over what she'd been writing. Alisa practically turned green.

"Uh, hi, Morgan," Mary K. said. There was a thin edge in her voice. Was it anger, or fear? I couldn't read her expression.

"What are you guys working on?" I asked.

"Oh," Mary K. said, glancing down at her paper. "Just a writing assignment." She shifted in her seat and glanced over my shoulder. "What are you doing here?"

I lifted my eyebrows. "I'm studying." I tried to get a better look at Mary K.'s notes. There seemed to be a lot of them. "You guys seem to be working pretty hard on this thing," I pressed, trying to make conversation.

Mary K. looked really uncomfortable. I turned to Alisa, who was as still as a stone. "Is it a project for class?" I asked. Alisa didn't respond. She stared down at the library table as if it were the most fascinating piece of wood in the universe.

I couldn't imagine what they'd be hiding from me. "What's going on?" I asked finally.

Mary K. stared helplessly at Alisa.

"Mary K. is helping me write a letter," Alisa said without looking up from the table. Then she raised her head and looked me in the eye. "It's to the town newspaper, and it's about the dangerous witchcraft going on around here."

She's lying. That was my first thought: She's lying—she'd never do that. And Mary K. would never help her. I turned to my sister. "Is this true?" I asked her.

Mary K. didn't reply.

"It was my idea," Alisa said, still looking at me with that defiant gaze.

"Mary K.?" My voice was a whisper. Mary K. wouldn't look at me.

"It was my idea," Alisa repeated.

I folded my arms across my chest. "Have I done something to you?" I asked her.

Alisa looked startled. "What?"

"Have I made you mad or something? Or has someone in Kithic done something wrong?" I struggled to hold my anger in check. Why was she doing this? What did she have to gain? "Because you seem to have turned against us."

"That—that's not true," Alisa insisted feebly.

"Isn't it?" I demanded. "Then what's the point of this letter?"

Alisa's mouth opened and closed. "It's just—it's just—" She groped for words. Finally she shook her head. "Look, forget it. Forget the letter. I'm not sending it."

"That doesn't answer my question," I pressed.

"Morgan," Mary K. said, "she just said that she isn't sending the letter. Isn't that enough?"

"I don't know," I said. I really didn't. I wanted to understand what was going on inside Alisa's head—but clearly she didn't want to let me in.

I looked at Mary K. "I guess I'll see you later."

She gave a quick nod and looked down at her paper again. I didn't say anything to Alisa, just turned and walked toward the stacks, fuming. Everything was skidding out of control lately—school, my family life, even my magick.

Just put it out of your mind, I told myself. You can always

talk to Mary K. later. I checked the call numbers of the books Erin had listed and realized they were on one of the top shelves. Grabbing a library ladder, I stepped up to the top rung and began hunting for the first title.

"Legacies of the Great Clans," I murmured to myself. "Legacies of—" My ladder tipped slightly, and I instinctively reached out and grabbed one of the shelves to keep myself from falling. It must be uneven, I thought as I wiggled myself gingerly to feel if the legs were stable. The ladder didn't move.

I didn't have time to think about that, though, because in a moment a book flew off the shelf, hurling itself against the books on the shelf across from it. Where have I seen that before? I wondered dimly as the entire bookcase began to rattle and shake. It gave a heavy groaning creak, and I looked back at it just in time to see it tip toward me.

I didn't even have time to let out a cry—I jumped from the ladder as the bookcase toppled. With a fierce crash, it slammed into the shelf across from it, and books slid off the shelves and thudded to the floor. I landed on the floor in a heap, under the tilted shelf, and felt a sharp pain in my shoulder. Around me there were shouts, then scuffling noises as people ran toward me.

"Are you okay?" The gangly librarian leaned over and helped me to my feet. She stared at the bookcase and the mess of books on the floor. "You could have been hurt!"

Staring at the wreckage, I started to shake. It was true. The bookshelf was massive and loaded with heavy volumes. If it had fallen completely, it could have landed on me. And if it had toppled the shelf across from it, it could have landed on someone else. I shuddered.

A small group of people had gathered nearby, and Erin pushed her way through them to come over to me. "What happened?" Her tone was sharp, her forehead creased with worry.

I cast a sideways glance at the librarian, who was inspecting the shelf gingerly. "It was just like the other day at Hunter's," I whispered. "I saw a book fly off the shelf before the whole thing toppled." Now I was shaking for real. Ciaran, I thought. It had to be him. Who else would—or could—do this? My birth father really was after me. Remembering what he had done to my mother, to her whole coven, I had to fight for breath. If Ciaran really was after me, how could I ever escape him?

I saw the muscles in Erin's jaw start to work. "How are you feeling?" she asked.

I felt my shoulder where I'd landed on it. "I'm okay," I said. "Just bruised."

"No," Erin said. "I mean, are you feeling lightheaded? Dizzy?" She frowned and passed a hand across my forehead. "Do you feel like you need to ground yourself?"

Suddenly I understood what she was saying. "You think *I* did this," I murmured.

Erin looked calmly at me. "Who do you think did it?" she asked.

Fear shot through me like lightning. "Ciaran," I said quickly.

"I don't think so." Erin's voice was certain, and I felt a flash of doubt. Could I have been responsible for this? I didn't think so. I would have felt the magick flowing through me, I reasoned.

"Do you have any idea how you summoned white witch fire when we were working together in Practical Magick?" Erin asked abruptly.

"No," I admitted.

"Morgan?" said a voice behind me. "My God, Morgan—are you okay?" It was Mary K. Alisa was right behind her.

"I'm fine," I said as Mary K. rushed over and gave me a hug. I winced at the pain in my shoulder but didn't complain.

"What happened?" Mary K. said as she eyed the shelf. I turned and stared back at the wreckage. *Someone could have been hurt,* screamed a voice in my brain. *Someone could have been killed!* "What were you doing, leaning on it or something?"

I shook my head but didn't say anything. Alisa was staring at Erin as if she were some kind of poisonous snake or tarantula. Her eyes darted from Erin to the shelf and finally settled on me. I felt I could almost see her mind working. She knows, I realized. She knows it's another magickal aberration. "Freak accident," Alisa said.

"Yes," Erin agreed. She looked at Alisa more closely. "Don't I know you?" she asked.

"We met last Saturday night," Alisa replied coolly. "At Hunter and Sky's."

Mary K.'s glance went to Erin, and she took an awkward step backward. I could see her putting the pieces together. Saturday night plus Hunter's house equals witchcraft. She looked back at me. "Aren't you here *to study?*" she asked sarcastically. Then she spun and stalked out of the library.

I started to go after her, but Erin held my arm in an iron grip.

"I'm glad you're okay," Alisa said quietly. Then she turned and went back to her table, where she started to gather her things.

I stared after her. "Morgan," Erin said, giving me a gentle

shake. I looked at her blankly. "Morgan, we need to have a circle. Right away."

"Circle?" I repeated dumbly.

Erin's face was pale and solemn. "This is becoming very serious," she said, indicating the fallen shelf. "We can't let it go on any longer."

"What do you mean?" I asked. I was afraid to hear the answer.

"I mean that we have to rein in your power right away," Erin replied. "Once you've learned more—once you're more in control of your magick—then we can do an unbinding spell. But right now, you're dangerous." She took my hand. "I'm sorry, Morgan."

I felt the air rush out of my lungs. *Dangerous.* The word echoed in my mind. "No," I wanted to say, "absolutely not." I thought about the white witch fire I had called up the other day. Erin was right; I had no idea where that power and knowledge had come from. Though it was different—I had felt myself channel the energy. Then I remembered the night the candle went out and the lightbulbs exploded. There could have been a fire. And now this. Mary K. was here, I thought. Mary K. could have been standing underneath that shelf.

My chest was tight. Erin was looking at me expectantly. "Okay," I said at last. "I'll do it."

8.
Loss

September 30, 1971

    It's been almost a week since it happened. I prepared the ritual, lit the fire in the cauldron, called upon the Goddess and the God for strength, and prepared to destroy Harris Stoughton's vile book. But I couldn't do it.

    It's hard to describe exactly what I was feeling. Fear, yes. And revulsion for the book and its author. But I also felt a strange sense of longing. I suppose it's my Rowanwand blood—the love of and hunger for knowledge that we are known for. At any rate, I simply couldn't destroy the book and take this knowledge—even though it's dark knowledge—out of the world forever. I had to find a safe place for it.

    My first thought was to bury it behind the house. Earth can be very powerful—it can purify objects that have been spelled. But I didn't want to run the risk that someone, or even some animal, might dig up the book and find it. Besides, the book itself hasn't been spelled. It's a book of dark spells, and there is no mountain of earth in the world that could purify it.

But I realized that there is a place in my very own house that is ringed with spells of obscurity . . . a secret place that no one but initiated blood witches can find: my parents' library. I decided to put it there for now and to warn them about the book as soon as possible. I hadn't wanted to tell them about it for fear of getting Sam into trouble. Then again, I thought that things had gone far enough.

My parents keep their dark magick titles, of which they have quite a few, on the highest shelf in the library. I had to get a stool to reach it. I stood there for a moment, reading the titles before me. Some of them were fairly chilling, and as I placed the Stoughton book among them, I had a deep sense of foreboding.

At the very moment that I slid the book in among the others, the reading lamp on the table in the corner began to rattle and shake. Then it started to move. Slowly at first, then gaining speed, it slid across the table and crashed to the floor. I squeezed my eyes shut tight. It's an earthquake, I thought, and I wanted to believe it—although whoever heard of an earthquake in Gloucester? Besides, I would have felt the whole room shaking.

Finally I managed to calm my breathing and opened my eyes. Everything was still, including the books on the top shelf. I left the library as quickly as possible and redrew the sigils in a hurry.

I was so scared that for a moment I considered doing a circle in my room to calm my nerves. But instead I went up to the widow's walk and let the rhythmic crashing of the waves hypnotize me.

I have to be honest with myself. Lately magick has seemed terrifying instead of wonderful. For now, I think I'll let nature be my religion.

—Sarah Curtis

"We have to go right now," Erin said, checking her watch. "Hunter should be home, and Sky is due back from the record store in twenty minutes. She may even be there by the time we arrive."

I nodded, mute. The incredible unspeaking Morgan. Part of me just couldn't believe that this was actually happening, and another part of me grasped that it was vitally important and had to take place right away. I found myself pulled along by the strength of Erin's will—following her like a stick caught in the current of the river.

Time seemed to slow down and everything around me felt surreal as Erin and I walked to my car. As I slid into my seat and turned the key in the ignition, I noticed that Erin's feet weren't touching the floor of the car. She looked ridiculously small on Das Boot's enormous bench seat, like a doll in an easy chair. Pulling into traffic, I felt hyperaware of the cars around me. Somehow a fly had found its way into my car, and it buzzed loudly against the windshield.

Erin's voice cut into my thoughts. "I won't lie to you, Morgan," she was saying. "The ceremony isn't going to be easy."

I interrupted her. "I've seen someone stripped of their powers," I said with a shudder, remembering David Redstone.

"It isn't like that," Erin said quickly. "It's unpleasant, but not at all like that. Reining puts limits on your powers, but it doesn't take them away. You'll still be able to do some small things, even some bigger things with the help of another, more powerful witch. And you can be unbound once you've gotten further in your training. Think of the reining as like a muzzle on a dog. Once the dog is taught not to bite, the muzzle can come off."

I gripped the steering wheel. "It sounds horrible," I said.

Erin turned and looked out the window. "It is," she said softly. "But Hunter and Sky and I will be there to make it as comfortable for you as we can."

Hunter. A small spark of hope flared in my chest and brought me back to reality. Hunter knew me—he knew I couldn't possibly be responsible for this. He would convince Erin that my magick didn't need to be reined. He would convince *me*.

He had to.

Sky was just striding up the front walk as we pulled into the driveway. She turned and gave us a little wave, as if she were happy to see us. Then we stepped out of the car and she saw our faces. Her smile vanished. Hunter appeared at the door. I guessed that he'd sensed us pull up.

"What is it?" Sky whispered to me as we walked up the front steps.

I didn't respond. No one said anything as we took off our coats and hats. Hunter went into the kitchen to put on a kettle for tea, and Erin, Sky, and I followed him. As I sat down at their table, I willed myself to relax.

"There's been another incident," Erin announced. "Morgan and I were in the library when books began to fly off the shelves, and the entire bookcase nearly crashed down on her head."

"Morgan?" Sky asked, leaning forward. Hunter turned pale.

"It would now seem that the common denominator for these incidents is Morgan," Erin went on. "I am concerned that if we allow her magick to remain unchecked, we run the risk of someone getting hurt."

"I don't think so." Hunter shook his head. "I'm almost certain that some of these incidents have been messages from my parents. I don't know how I know it, but I feel it's true."

"Did you feel that what happened at the circle on Saturday was a message from your parents?" Erin asked.

I felt my heart beat once. Twice. Three times. "No," Hunter replied.

"And this latest incident in the library wouldn't have been, either," Erin went on. "Hunter," she said in a gentler tone, "it's possible that you are receiving messages from your parents. What happened when we scried and what you described at the movie theater, even the figure in the fog—those things *do* sound like messages. It's also possible that Morgan is causing these telekinetic incidents and that they're entirely unrelated to what you've experienced. You've said yourself that she has very strong powers and that she isn't a very skilled witch . . . yet."

"I don't know." Sky spoke up, surprising me. "Skilled or not, it seems to me that if Morgan was doing this, she'd feel it."

I felt so grateful to her that I almost leapt up and hugged her.

"Who, then?" Erin demanded.

"Ciaran," Hunter suggested.

Erin scoffed. "Hunter, you know as well as I do that proximity is important for telekinesis, even for a witch as strong as Ciaran. He has to be near her. He wouldn't be able to control books in a library in Widow's Vale when he's in Spain—it's impossible."

"Well, you were at both Saturday's circle and at the library, Erin," I snapped. "And those have been the only two telekinetic incidents so far."

Erin cocked an eyebrow. "Have they?" she demanded.

My mind whirled, and I felt sick as I remembered my books leaping from my locker and scattering all over the floor. "Maybe not," I admitted.

Sky raised her eyebrows, and Erin leaned back in her chair. Hunter dug his hands into the pockets of his black corduroys. I told them briefly about my locker.

I expected Hunter to ask why I hadn't told him about this before. But he didn't. He just turned and gazed out the window for a long time.

It was Sky who broke the silence. "So—what should we do?" she asked.

"I think Morgan's power needs to be reined." Erin looked from Hunter to Sky. "Now. This evening."

Sky looked at Hunter.

"That ritual isn't to be done lightly," he said to the window.

"Are you willing to risk it?" Erin demanded. "Someone could have been killed today. *Morgan* could have been killed."

Hunter turned and looked at me. His eyes were full of pain. Tell her, I wanted to shout. Tell her that it isn't me! But what he said was, "I'm sorry, Morgan."

There was a long creak as Sky pushed her chair away from the table. "I've got some white clothes upstairs," she said. "Come, Morgan."

I couldn't believe this was happening—that Hunter was letting this happen. I blinked fast, trying to clear my eyes of bitter tears. I wanted to scream, to shout, but what could I say? I tried to imagine how I would feel if I refused to let my powers be reined and then something horrible happened, but it was too awful to think about.

It's only temporary, I told myself as I followed Sky upstairs to her room. I tried really hard to believe it.

When I came downstairs, wearing Sky's white tunic and pants, Hunter had already drawn a circle. At its center was a large, heavy-looking stone basin, filled with water. Thick, pungent incense saturated the air. It was a kind I'd never smelled before, and it had a dark, earthy quality that reminded me of caves and dense forests. The sun had sunk quickly, and the only light in the room came from a few flickering candles.

I stepped inside the circle, and Hunter drew it closed. Each of us stood by one of the four corners—Hunter by earth, Sky by air, Erin by water, and I by fire.

In a low voice Erin began to chant. The words were Gaelic, strange and ancient-sounding.

Acarach ban-dia
Acarach dia
Do cumhachd, do aofrom
Séol lamh
Bann treòir

The water in the basin began to shimmer and glow. For a moment it looked like a pool of liquid gold. Then a light flared from the center of it—small yet brilliant, like a lump of coal that burned as bright as the sun. I couldn't look directly at it. After a moment the coal sent up a column of light bright enough to bathe the entire room in dazzling whiteness. The column was shot through with glowing sparks, specks of silver confetti.

I felt a similar spark rise in my chest—a brilliant light was growing within me. I felt wonderfully, powerfully alive. My heart leapt, and I wanted to shout, "It's beautiful!" but in the next moment something happened that made my skin turn cold.

Ugly black smoke began to pour from the bottom of the basin. It was thick and heavy and rolled along the floor. It had gone no more than two feet in all directions from the basin when it slowly began to rise. But it didn't rise the way normal smoke does, floating on the air through the room. Instead it rose like bars, or long wicked fingers, around the light. It rose until it reached the ceiling, then closed around the light like a dark clutching claw.

My lungs felt tight. I struggled for air. The brilliant light within me was dimming, held in the clutches of the horrible blackness. I fell to my knees.

Hunter, Sky, and Erin began chanting. After a moment the

pain in my chest receded and I could breathe, although I felt very sick. The black fingers pulled the brilliant column of light down, slowly, into the bowl, until it was nothing but a swirling pool of gray streaked with flashes of light, like a tiny dark sky full of lightning. The chanting stopped, and I knew that Hunter, Sky, and Erin had done their best to help me. Still, my head was throbbing and I had to choke down the bile that rose in my throat.

For a moment the room was completely still.

"Morgan." Hunter strode over to me and tried to help me to my feet.

I shook him off. "I'm fine."

A hurt look crossed his face, but I didn't apologize. I stood up, my knees nearly buckling.

"Morgan, you should eat something," Erin suggested.

The thought of food repulsed me. Besides, I was dying to get out of there. Right now I couldn't look at any of them— not even Hunter. "I'll eat at home," I said weakly. I checked my watch and nearly gasped. Seven-thirty! Oh my God— family night was supposed to start at six! I remembered how excited my mother had been earlier that day, and a new wave of nausea rolled through me. I couldn't believe I'd just let my mom down in order to participate in this horrible ceremony. "I have to go," I said, and took a staggering step toward the stairs. Sky swooped toward me, but I held up my hand. "I'm fine," I insisted. "Let me do this."

I gritted my teeth and somehow managed to make it upstairs and change into my normal clothes. By the time I came back downstairs, I was feeling a bit clearer, although the headache was exquisitely painful.

"I'll drive you," Hunter offered, but I shook my head.

"I've got Das Boot," I snapped. "Don't worry, I'll make it home fine."

I turned to leave, but Hunter said, "Morgan." The pain in his voice made me turn around, and I forced myself to face him. Hunter looked pale and worried, and I realized suddenly that he really hadn't wanted to do this any more than I had.

"Call me later," was all he said. He put his hand on my shoulder.

"Okay," I said, but our gazes remained locked for a moment longer. His green eyes communicated a world of thoughts and feelings. He loved me. He was afraid for me. He didn't want anything to happen to me.

I held that look in my heart the entire drive home. It was the only thing that made me feel even a little bit better.

"Where have you been?" my mother demanded the minute I walked in the door. No, "Hello," no, "Are you all right?" She was sitting on the couch with her arms folded across her chest. The headache threatened to split my skull in two.

I put my fingers to my left temple and rubbed it. "I'm sorry—" I began.

"Not good enough," my mom snapped. "What is going on, Morgan?"

I didn't know how to answer her. I just stood there, a lump in the living room.

My mom threw her hands up. "What am I supposed to do?" she asked. "What? You knew that family night was important to me—yet not only did you blow it off, you didn't even phone to tell me you weren't coming." She pushed herself off the couch and faced me. "Tell me how to get through to you, Morgan," she said. "What's left?"

I didn't know what to tell her. There was no way I could make her understand what had happened tonight, and I didn't really even *want* her to know. The accident at the library, the reining of my powers—it was too scary for me to deal with, never mind my mom. "I don't know," I mumbled.

"Well, that makes two of us." My mom sighed, then said, "I'm sorry, but I just can't take much more of this. I've tried reaching out to you; now I'm going to try punishing you. You're grounded."

I opened my mouth to protest but thought better of it. She was right.

"Okay," I said.

"I mean it, Morgan," she went on. "No phone, no television, no going out—nothing but schoolwork for the next two weeks."

I closed my eyes. I still felt thoroughly awful. "Okay."

"Look at me," my mom said, so I opened my eyes. "I love you," she said. Her voice wasn't sentimental—she was just stating a fact. "And I don't understand what's going on. But whatever it is, I'm not going to let it take my daughter away from me, is that clear?"

I nodded. "Yeah," I said. There was a beat of silence.

"I'm finished," my mom said finally. "For now."

I turned to go upstairs but stopped suddenly. "Mom?"

"Yes?" She sounded tired.

"I really am sorry," I said. The words hung there a

moment, but she didn't reply. I trudged toward the stairs. Every muscle in my body—every fiber—ached. My head was pounding, and my heart was heavy. I pictured Hunter in my mind, tried to visualize the look he had given me just before I left. Only this time, instead of making me feel better, it made me feel worse. I wanted to call him. I needed to hear his voice. But now it was impossible—I was grounded.

I lay on my bed, and the pain in my head dulled a little. I wondered about the limits of my magick now that I was reined. Erin had said that I would still be able to do some small spells. Could I send him a witch message? I wondered. I decided to give it a try. *Hunter,* I thought, *Hunter. I need you.*

I felt echoing emptiness inside me and knew it wasn't working. But I tried again, anyway. And again. And again. Even though there was no reply, I didn't give up. I couldn't.

I didn't know what else to do.

9.
Fear

I passed Bree in The hall Today. I said hello, buT she didn'T hear me.

AT leasT, I <u>Think</u> she didn'T hear me. She looked kind of preoccupied, buT maybe ThaT was jusT an acT so ThaT she could preTend noT To noTice me. I'm sure Morgan Told her abouT me quiTTing KiThic.

I haven'T even missed a circle yeT, buT already There are so many Things I miss abouT The coven. I miss The energy I felT from being parT of The circle. I miss The feeling when a circle goes well and you feel like There's a greaTer power in The room wiTh you. Like everyone's energy has combined and formed This force ThaT's more powerful Than The sum of iTs parTs. I miss feeling like I have a family.

Well, whaTever—who cares? I'm noT in The coven anymore. WhaT They do is Their own problem. I'm noT going To Try To warn anyone abouT anyThing—I'm sTaying ouT of iT. I did my besT. From now on, This is jusT a journal, not a Book of Shadows. And I'm just a high school sophomore, not a Witch in Training.

I would have made a Terrible witch, anyway. I don't have The stomach for it.

—Alisa

"Morgan, what is that?" Jenna asked, peering at the bowl of steaming hot something I'd gotten from the cafeteria. It was lunch period the next day, and I was sitting with Sharon, Raven, Jenna, Matt, Bree, Robbie, and Ethan. Lately I'd been spending almost all of my lunch periods in the library in a desperate attempt to pull my grades up, but today I simply felt too sick to concentrate on anything. I looked around at the familiar faces. If my grades didn't improve, I might be eating lunch at an entirely different school soon.

"Chili," I said. "I think."

"Isn't that the same stuff they served Monday?" Matt asked.

I gave him a wry half smile, but Bree let out a silky laugh. Matt grinned at her. Jenna glanced up and gave me a wary look across the table. What was Bree up to?

"You have to give the school credit on their food-recycling program," Raven said. "No one can bear to eat it, but no one can bear to let it go to waste."

Robbie was sitting next to me on one side of the table with Jenna. Sharon and Ethan were on the other, and Matt was at one of the short ends, sandwiched between Bree and Raven. He looked like he was in heaven. Bree and Robbie, on the other hand, hadn't exchanged a single word during lunch, and now Robbie was staring down at his sandwich as if he thought he could make it disintegrate with the power of his mind.

"So is everybody going to make it this Saturday?" Sharon asked. Kithic was holding its circle at her house.

"I can't go," I said, feeling even gloomier. "I'm grounded."

"Grounded? What did you do?" Ethan asked, pushing curly hair out of his eyes. "Anything good?"

"Unfortunately not."

"Morgan isn't much good at being bad." Bree gave Matt a flirtatious little smile. "Unlike some people."

"Hmmm," Raven said smoothly. "Tell us about that, Bree."

Bree ignored her, still looking at Matt, who was grinning like an idiot. I narrowed my eyes at Bree. What did she think she was doing?

Robbie stood up. "I've gotta head to the library," he said to nobody in particular. "See you guys later." He grabbed his tray and walked off.

I caught Bree's eye and frowned at her. She made a face at me. "I'll be right back," I said, pushing my chair away from the table.

Robbie was halfway down the hall by the time I caught up with him. "Robbie, wait," I said, catching his arm. "What's going on?"

"I don't know." His eyes were filled with anger. "I guess I just didn't feel like sitting around and watching Bree hit on someone else. Call me crazy."

I folded my arms across my chest and cocked an eyebrow. "I thought you guys were broken up."

Robbie looked shocked. I knew it, I thought.

"That's what Bree told me, anyway," I went on. "She said you dumped her."

Robbie's eyes were wide. "What are you talking about?" he demanded.

I shrugged. "Isn't that what happened?"

"No," he insisted. "No way!" He looked confused and worried. "I just told Bree that I thought we needed some space. We've been spending all our time together lately, and . . . well . . . I've gotten these weird vibes from Bree. Like she's feeling kind of . . ."

"Possessive?" I finished for him.

"Yeah." He nodded. "So I tried to talk to her about it. I mean, look, personally I'd love to spend all my time with Bree. But it seemed sort of weird for *her*. Don't forget that I've known Bree a long time."

"As long as I have."

"Exactly," Robbie agreed. "And we both know she gets bored easily with guys, and then she moves on. Right?"

"Mmm." Dead right.

"So I thought I'd be clever and suggest more space," Robbie explained, "and she's been avoiding me ever since. I thought she was just taking me up on my offer." He bit his lip. "God, Morgan, have I totally screwed up?"

"I don't think it's your fault, but the situation is definitely screwed up," I said. "You have to talk to her. Now."

"What should I say?"

"Just tell her that this is all a big misunderstanding, which it is," I said. "Look, Robbie, you and I both know that underneath it all, Bree is actually insecure in a weird way, right?"

"About some things," he admitted.

"About this thing," I said. "This has just gotten blown out of proportion because she actually cares about you. A lot. And she doesn't know how to deal."

Robbie looked dubious. "You think?"

"I know it," I told him. I didn't think it was betraying a confidence to say that much. "So you'll talk to her?" I asked.

"Yeah," he said. He started to turn back toward the lunch-room, but the bell rang. "Damn," he said, checking his watch.

"Do it after school," I said as people began trickling into the hall. "Don't wait."

"Thanks, Morgan." Robbie reached out and drew me into a hug. I felt glad that I'd finally butted in. My head was still throbbing, but it was good to know that I'd done at least one thing right.

I was halfway through my first problem set when the doorbell rang. "Mary K., can you get that?" I shouted. My head was still splitting, even after I'd taken four Advil. Mary K. didn't reply. Not surprising. She was playing the radio at top volume in her room. I had expected her to be at cheer-leading practice, but it had been canceled at the last minute. Now she was upstairs "studying" with her new best friend, Alisa. They were in the same French class.

With a sigh, I hauled myself up from the dining-room table and trudged to the door, figuring it was probably some-one from Greenpeace or another member of the Mary K. fan club. The latter was more likely.

I looked through the peephole and sucked in my breath. Erin! I'd completely forgotten we were supposed to meet to go over what I'd read about witch history. Crap. And now I *had* to answer the door. She was a witch, after all—she knew I was here.

"Hello, Morgan," she said. Her dark red hair was pulled into a braid, and she was carrying a backpack. In blue jeans and a peacoat, she looked more like a Vassar student than a forty-seven-year-old witch.

"Hi," I said, looking nervously behind her. My mom and dad weren't due home for a couple of hours, but I didn't want to take any chances. I wasn't supposed to have any visitors, and I knew that if they caught me with Erin, I was toast.

Erin cocked an eyebrow. "May I come in?" she asked.

"Actually . . . ," I said, pulling the door closed behind me. "I've sort of been grounded. For coming home late. I'm not supposed to have any visitors. I'm just supposed to go to school and come home—no TV, no phone, nothing."

"I see." Erin's face was a neutral blank. "And how long is this going to last?"

I grimaced. "Two weeks."

"I see," Erin said again. We stood there, staring at each other for a few moments. She made no move to leave.

I cleared my throat. "So you see, I'm not supposed to have any visitors," I began again. "Um, my parents are actually thinking about sending me to a Catholic school. So I'm trying to pull my grades up. They might change their minds."

"Yes, I can appreciate that," Erin replied. "But the fact is, Morgan, that I'm only going to be here for a short time. Do you take my meaning?"

I wavered. Erin was right. I was having a rough time familywise, but she'd come all the way from Scotland and so far hadn't had much of a chance to teach me anything. Something always seemed to get in the way. If I didn't let her in today, her entire trip would be pretty much of a wash.

"I brought you some more books," Erin said, pulling off

her backpack. "A few from my own collection on Irish witches in the medieval period."

"Well," I said slowly, "I am writing a paper on the persecution of witches."

"Then it's a school project, isn't it?" Erin blinked at me innocently.

That did it. "Come in," I said quickly, leading her into the front hall. "But my sister is home, so we'll have to be careful."

"Oh, don't worry about me. I won't make a peep," Erin promised. Then she cast a quick see-me-not spell so that Mary K. wouldn't see or hear her as she slipped up the stairs. Not that there was much danger of that, considering the volume of the music pulsing from Mary K.'s room.

"Sorry it's such a mess," I said as I brushed a pile of clothes from my bed to the floor. Dagda, my gray kitten, had been sleeping at the foot of the bed. He stretched and mewed a mild complaint. Erin walked over to him and scratched him under the chin.

"He's a cute one," she said as Dagda stretched his neck and purred contentedly.

I smiled. Dagda had grown quite a bit since I'd first gotten him. Now he was looking like a lanky teenager of a cat, with gangly legs and paws that seemed enormous in proportion to the rest of him. Lately he spent all of his time either sleeping or dashing around the house madly—usually in the middle of the night.

Erin dropped her backpack and turned to look at me. "Have you finished *Legacies of the Great Clans?*" she asked.

I groaned. "Not even half of it," I admitted.

Erin studied my face a moment. "How are you feeling?"

"Like crap," I said bluntly. "I've got a headache that I can't get rid of." I ran my thumb along the ridge of my right eye.

"A stabbing pain?" she asked. "Like a knife to the skull?"

That was exactly what it felt like. "Pretty much," I agreed.

"And your breathing is a little tight? Your chest is heavy?" Erin suggested.

I nodded. "Is that normal?" I asked.

"Unfortunately." Erin took my wrist and felt for my pulse. She seemed to think for a moment, then said, "I'm sorry, Morgan. I know this isn't easy for you."

It was strange. I had gotten so used to magick flowing through me that right now I was feeling like a clogged drain— something less than useless. I remembered when I had first met Cal and my magick had begun to reveal itself. I'd felt frightened and off-kilter. Now I just felt . . . hollow.

"Before we begin, I think we should do a little meditation," Erin went on. "It should clear your head and make the pain recede."

I went and dug my altar out of my closet. Erin lit the candle and the incense, and I drew a circle on the floor and turned out the overhead light. It was gray and cloudy outside, so the room was fairly dark. Dagda stalked over to the altar to investigate, sniffed everything, then dashed away at top speed. I opened the door and let him out, then sat on the floor, facing Erin, my back to the bathroom that connected my room with Mary K.'s.

Erin reached out and took my hands in hers. Her fingers were cool and smooth, and the minute we touched, I felt strength and comfort flowing from her. We didn't speak, but soon I felt magick pulsing through the room.

Clear your mind. I heard the words although Erin hadn't spoken. I closed my eyes and tried to reach out. An image flashed in my brain—Erin standing before me in a yellow field, wearing a brilliant blue dress made of a delicate fabric, embroidered with symbols older than any I knew. *Let go of the pain.* Erin reached out to me, and the fabric of her ancient dress rustled in the breeze.

At her touch, the stabbing pain in my forehead dulled a bit. My head was still throbbing, but it was a muted ache. My chest lifted, and I took a deep breath of clean air. I felt infinitely better.

I smiled at her, and she smiled back.

Just then I felt something slam me in the back. I let out a startled cry and heard someone shriek behind me. I opened my eyes to see Erin falling away from me. Everything, the floor, the altar, everything was falling away. Erin's grip tightened on my hands, and my arm muscles tensed as I tried desperately not to let go. For a dizzy moment I expected Erin to shout at me not to let her drop.

"Oh my God!" the person behind me screamed. I turned and saw it was Alisa. Her face was white and covered in a light film of sweat. She looked confused, like she wasn't quite sure where she was. But something about her orientation was wrong. She was standing, supporting herself against the door frame to the bathroom. And I was sitting, yet my face was almost level with hers.

"Oh my God!" she screamed again, her eyes wide with horror. That was when I understood what was happening. *I was levitating.*

My heart clenched in a cold fist of fear. I was going to

fall! I flailed with my legs but only succeeded in kicking the bathroom door shut. My hair fell forward over my shoulders. "Don't let go!" I screamed to Erin. "Don't let go of me!" In my panic I pictured myself flattened against the ceiling of my room, crushed by the weight of reverse gravity.

Erin closed her eyes and made a low humming noise at the back of her throat. I felt myself sinking slowly, an inch, then another, toward the floor.

Alisa's face was greenish white. She backed away from me, then ran toward the door that led into the hall. I heard her footsteps thudding on the stairs and saw a gray streak as Dagda dashed after her.

"What's going on?" I heard Mary K. shout. Somewhere in the back of my mind it registered that her music wasn't playing anymore.

I got lower, and lower. . . . Finally I was only a few inches off the floor. All at once I dropped onto my jute rug in a sprawling heap.

I looked up at Erin. "That wasn't me," I said.

"I know," she said. I looked at her closely and realized that she was afraid.

I heard Mary K.'s footsteps on the stairs, then the front door slamming. All at once there was a squeal of tires and a piercing scream.

Mary K.! I scrambled to my feet and nearly flew down the stairs, Erin right behind me. I dashed out onto the muddy front lawn and came to a stop by Mary K., who was standing perfectly still in the middle of the front walk, her hand covering her mouth. Alisa's dark form was retreating down the street—she was running home, I guessed. But that wasn't what Mary K. was looking at. I followed her gaze and saw that she was staring at a car that had stopped in front of our house. The door opened, and a heavyset woman rushed out and peered at something next to her front fender.

At first I thought that she had hit a piece of wood or some garbage in the road. Then I saw the thing move. One gray paw twitched feebly.

Dagda.

My heart clutched. The woman looked up and saw us. "Help!" she cried. Tears began to rain down her cheeks. "Oh God, I'm so sorry! I love cats." She looked at me helplessly. "He just came out of nowhere."

I couldn't speak. I bent mutely over Dagda.

The woman began crying even harder. "I'm so sorry," she said again.

Dagda's eyes opened, then closed again. He was alive! But though there wasn't any blood on him, I could see at a glance that he was badly hurt. I tried to cast my senses, but it was no use. My magick was still reined.

My vision blurred with helpless tears. I turned around and saw Erin behind me. She bent and studied my kitten for a moment. "The injuries are internal," she said. Her voice was low, but I could tell from her expression that Dagda was dying.

I didn't know what to do. I didn't want to move him for fear of causing him more pain. Tears spilled down my cheeks as I looked at him, his fur matted and soaked with gray left-over snow.

I couldn't just let him lie there, die there, in the street. I picked him up, cradling him in my arms.

Mary K. was still frozen to her spot on the front walk.

"Morgan," Erin said. She leaned toward Dagda, and I wanted to scream at her to get away from him, to leave him alone, but I couldn't. Her hand hovered hesitantly over Dagda, her face questioning.

Then I remembered. Erin is a healer, I thought. I could feel the movement of Dagda's tiny lungs as he labored to breathe. I started to sob wrenchingly. Could she heal him? Surely he was too far gone, even for a witch's power.

Erin squeezed my shoulder. Once again strength seemed to flow from her into me. "Quiet yourself," she said gently. "Don't let your emotions control you."

I took a deep breath. Then another. Erin's strength flowed through my body. I said nothing as she lowered her hand and touched Dadga's head. She stroked him tenderly, with the force of a butterfly's wings. Closing her eyes, she stood without moving. Time seemed to stand still, and I held my breath. I don't know how long we stood there like that— it might have been five minutes or five hours.

Dagda let out a small mew.

"Oh thank God," the heavyset woman said. "Oh, thank you, Lord! I thought I'd killed him!"

Erin's face was serious. "He's badly hurt," she said, then turned to me. "You should get him to a veterinarian as soon as possible."

"I know a good one," I said, thinking of my aunt's girl-friend, Paula Steen. Her clinic was the closest one I knew of—only about fifteen minutes away. "Thank you," I said, and Erin nodded.

I don't know why, but I turned to the heavyset woman and said, "He's going to be fine."

"Bless you," she replied, which struck me as odd, but sort of sweet and strangely appropriate.

Still cradling Dagda with one arm, I pulled my keys out of my pocket and turned toward my car. Then I heard a voice call, "Morgan?"

It was Mary K. She looked lost. "Can I come with you?" she asked.

I didn't even have to think. "Let's go," I said.

10.
Confrontation

October 3, 1971

I finally worked up the nerve to warn my mother about the book, but she hardly seemed interested, let alone worried. I told her that the powers of Wicca were starting to seem uncontrollable to me—and frightening in a way that they never had before.

Mother didn't like that. She laid down her knife and told me that I was being "ignorant." She made it sound like she thought I was a hysteric—like those people during the witch trials. Another Harris Stoughton.

I told her that I had some good reasons to be freaked out, but she just said that she didn't want to hear it. She said that we were responsible witches and that we had a right to our beliefs.

Just at that very moment—I mean <u>exactly</u> as she

said that—the silverware drawer flew out. It just flew right out of the cabinet and landed on the floor with a clatter. Then an icy wind blew through the room and the cabinet doors burst open.

"Get down!" Mother yelled as the plates flew out and hurtled against the wall—crash crash crash!

I screamed and screamed until the cupboard was empty. I screamed until my mother picked herself off the floor and took me by the shoulders. She shook me, but my scream went on and on until I couldn't scream anymore.

Then Mother held me and told me that everything would be all right. But I don't believe her.

There is dark magick in this house. For a while I thought it was the book itself that was responsible, but I know that's impossible. It's just a book. It may be full of evil, but it can't actually make things happen.

I can hardly bear to think it, but I have to. Could Sam have been behind it?

—Sarah Curtis

"May I help you?" the woman behind the desk asked as I rushed into the veterinary clinic. She was middle-aged with dyed blond hair and looked bored.

"I'm here to see Paula," I said in a rush. "Doctor Steen."

"Do you have an appointment?" the receptionist asked.

"No, I—" Just then Mary K. walked in with Dagda in her arms. The woman took one look at Dagda and said, "Come with me."

We followed her down a long white hallway and into a small room. "Just a minute." The woman hurried out of the room. Barely a minute had passed before Paula walked in.

"Morgan!" She looked surprised and pleased. "Mary K.!" A quick glance at Dagda and her smile evaporated. "What happened?" she asked.

"He was hit by a car," I said as Mary K. laid Dagda gently on the steel table at the center of the room. Dagda struggled to get up but couldn't.

Paula pursed her lips. She palpated Dagda's ribs and stomach gently. Then she touched his left foreleg and frowned. "This needs an X ray," she said.

"Is he going to be all right?" Mary K. asked nervously.

Paula looked at her and smiled reassuringly. "This is one lucky kitty," she said. "I think his leg is broken. He might have to hobble around on a cast for a while, but all things considered, that's pretty minor."

I exhaled with relief. "That's great news," I said.

"Why don't you guys wait outside while I take the X ray?" she suggested. "If we do have to put a cast on, we may have to sedate him. It could take a little while."

I threw myself into one of the large, comfortable chairs in the waiting room while Mary K. went outside to the pay phone to let our parents know where we were. I was glad we had come here. I didn't know where the receptionist was, but she was no longer behind her desk. I was alone in the waiting room as the sky outside grew from pink to dusky gray and the shadows disappeared.

What had happened today? I dug a hand into my pocket, remembering the feeling of the door slamming into my back, the fear as I left the ground, Alisa's screams. Thank the Goddess that Erin was there, I thought. She saw everything. She knows I couldn't have levitated myself. Especially not with my power restrained the way it is.

But then, who did it?

There was a sudden blast of cold air as Mary K. stepped back into the clinic. "I finally reached Mom," she reported. "She said she hopes Dagda's okay and she's glad we thought to go to Paula."

"Thanks, Mary K.," I said.

"I called Alisa, too," Mary K. said, sliding into the seat next to mine. "But her dad said she's too sick to come to the phone." Mary K.'s voice told me that she wasn't exactly sure this story was true. She looked at me sideways. "What happened in there?" she asked. "Why did she run out of our house?"

I sighed. "I'm really not sure." It was the truth. "I'm not sure why she came bursting into my room in the first place."

Mary K. shrugged. "She wasn't feeling great. Maybe she just got confused which door was which."

I thought about Alisa's face, distorted in fear. "She doesn't like me."

"She doesn't know you," Mary K. replied. After a moment she added, "And you don't know her."

Something in her tone of voice made me look at her. "What do you mean?" I asked.

Mary K. sighed. "It's just—Alisa's going through some pretty rough family things right now. She's not . . . not at her best."

I sank back into the chair, wondering what was going on with Alisa. But Mary K. clearly didn't want to tell me, and I didn't want to press her for details. Suddenly I felt guilty for not reaching out to Alisa more. It was obvious that she was troubled and that probably the animosity she felt toward me didn't really have anything to do with me.

Still, at least she had a friend like Mary K. Someone who didn't give up secrets easily. Someone who cared. I gave my sister a sideways look, loving her. I really hoped we could get past the trouble we were having now.

Paula came out with Dagda in her arms. He was wearing a small cast on his foreleg, which stuck out awkwardly from the rest of his limbs. "Here you go," Paula singsonged. "Good as new—or almost. He's a little out of it from the sedation, but that'll wear off by morning."

I rushed over, and Paula handed Dagda to me. He stirred in my arms, and Mary K. scratched him behind the ears. "Thank you so much, Paula," I said. Dagda's breathing was perfectly normal, and he didn't seem to be in any pain. And thank you, Erin, I added silently.

"It's just a fracture. You'll need to come back in two weeks so we can check on his progress," Paula said. "But I think we'll be able to take the cast off then."

We said good-bye, and I handed Dagda to Mary K. so I could drive. On the way home Mary K. asked, "Who was that woman who was at the house today? She was the same one you were at the library with, right?"

I winced. I should have seen this question coming. "She's a tutor."

"And a witch, right?" Mary K. asked.

"Anyone who has been initiated into a coven is a witch," I replied, figuring that a half-truth is better than no truth at all.

Mary K. stroked Dagda. "So—why are you hanging out

with her?" Her voice held a distinct note of unease.

"She's teaching me."

"Like, how to put hexes on people and stuff?" Mary K. asked.

"No," I said curtly. Hadn't she learned anything about Wicca from being around me? "Of course not. She's teaching me about the history of Wicca and about herbs."

Mary K. looked dubious. "Herbs?"

"Herbs have a lot of medicinal properties. Some can speed recovery. I mean, there might even be something I could feed Dagda that would make him get better sooner."

"Really?" She sounded intrigued. "I wonder if she could help Alisa. She's been sort of worn out lately."

"Do you want me to ask Erin about it?" I suggested.

"No," Mary K. said quickly. "No, don't."

I didn't press her. Out of the corner of my eye I watched as she rubbed Dagda's belly and he purred sleepily. She had been there when Erin healed Dagda—but how much had she actually understood? I was afraid to find out.

When we got home, Mary K. handed Dagda over to me, and I took him upstairs and settled him comfortably on my bed. He instantly dozed off once I put him down.

"How is he?"

I turned around and saw my mom standing in my doorway. "He's fine," I said, giving Dagda a small pat. Mom came over and gave him a gentle rub on the head. "Paula says the cast can come off in two weeks."

"That's good news." My mom's eyes lingered on Dagda a moment, then she turned to me. "Come downstairs, Morgan. Your father and I want to talk to you."

I felt my throat tighten, but I followed her downstairs to where my father was sitting on the couch with his serious face on. My mom sat down beside him. I took the armchair across from them—The Accused.

"Morgan, Mary K. told us that you had a visitor today," my mom began. "And that you were with a friend in the library yesterday."

My body went cold. I tried to read my mother's face— did she know that Erin was a witch? I didn't think so.

"You weren't supposed to have any visitors," my mom went on. "You knew the rules, and you broke them."

I wanted to protest, but I knew that would only make things worse. I clamped my lips together and sat on my hands.

"Morgan, your father and I have talked about this a great deal. We want you to be in a supportive environment. We don't want you to throw your future away. You need guidance and a firm hand and—"

Fear gnawed at my stomach like a hungry rat. No. This couldn't be. "What are you saying?" I asked.

"What your mother is saying," my dad put in, "is that we think it would be best if you went to Saint Anne's starting at the beginning of next quarter."

Oh, no, no, no! My stomach fell. "What?" I cried.

My mother's nostrils flared. "Look, we've given you a number of chances to show us that you're turning your grades around, and you've disobeyed us at every step. This started long ago—back when we asked you not to read Wiccan books—"

"So that's it," I broke in, stunned. "You're sending me to a Catholic school to try to convert me!"

"What?" My mom looked shocked.

"Morgan, don't be ridiculous," my father said. "We just want what's best for you."

"And what's best for me is Catholicism and not Wicca, right?" I shot back. "I can't possibly have both in my life."

"You were raised with Catholic values," my mom said hotly. "Those are *our* values."

I stood up and faced them. "Look, I can't help being a witch," I said. My voice shook. "Wicca is in my blood. I couldn't change it even if I wanted to. But that's the point—I *don't* want to. I respect your beliefs. Why can't you live with mine?"

The minute the words were out of my mouth, I wanted to call them back. My father's face went white, and my heart ached, but it was too late. My parents sat on the couch, stone-faced and silent. It was so quiet that I could hear the seconds ticking by on my watch.

Then my mom stood up. "Morgan, we've made this decision already. We want to put you in a positive environment—and we found one that seemed to offer the kind of academic support and discipline we think you need. We want you to value school and excel in it as you have in the past. I'm sorry if that offends you, but it's something else you're going to have to live with." She turned and walked out of the room.

My father stood and faced me. "We love you," he said in a quiet voice. He took off his glasses and pinched the bridge of his nose, and I saw in his eyes that my father was afraid—afraid for me.

We looked at each other a moment, then he turned and followed my mom.

"I love you, too," I said softly to the empty room.

11.
Connection

I'm scared. I think I might be going crazy.

Today I was over at Mary K.'s house, and I started to feel sick—kind of dizzy and nauseated. So I went to her bathroom to splash water on my face.

While I was standing at the sink, something weird started to happen. My hearing started to fade, almost as if someone had stuffed wads of cotton in my ears, and then my vision started to narrow, like I was looking through a tube. I thought I was starting to black out, so I sat on the toilet seat and put my head between my knees. After a few minutes I felt a little better, so I got up and splashed a little more water on my face. Then I headed out through the door—only I guess I got the wrong one because I walked into Morgan's room, and there she was doing some bizarre ritual with Erin. That's when things started to get really crazy. I think I started hallucinating because I thought I saw Morgan rise into

The air, like some kind of freaky scene from <u>The Exorcist</u>.

Needless to say, I got out of there. But I still don't know if what I saw was real.

And I can't figure out what would be more frightening—if it was, or if it wasn't.

—Alisa

It was a dismal morning—gray and chilly—and I kept my head down and my shoulders hunched as I strode toward the quiet school building. The bell had rung ten minutes ago. Mary K. had always made sure that I was up by seven-thirty, but now that she was barely speaking to me, I didn't have any more wake-up insurance. Today I was late beyond all redemption, thanks to the fact that I'd overslept by forty-five minutes. I was still feeling headachy and ill, and the weather made me feel even worse. The absence of my magick was so overpowering that it was almost like a presence. I couldn't wait to get inside the warm school and distract myself with academics for a while. Or maybe I could catch a few winks in English class. Since I'd be attending Saint Anne's soon, I could afford to catch a nap here and there while I could.

Morgan.

I spun around. Who's calling me? I thought. But of course, my magick was still reined. Apparently I could still receive a witch message—I just couldn't send one. I turned back and scanned the front of the building.

At first I didn't see him. I had to look very closely before I noticed Hunter standing beside the large oak tree that grew to the far right of the building.

"How are you?" he asked as I walked up to him. His navy blue cap was pulled down over his hair, and the wind had made his cheeks pink. "You look tired."

"I'm okay," I said. "Listen, Hunter, I know I said I'd call you the other day—"

"Morgan, it's fine," he interrupted me. "I knew you wouldn't be able to send a witch message, and Erin explained that you were grounded. She told me a few other things, too." Hunter reached out and pulled me into his arms. "I'm so glad you're all right," he whispered into my hair.

I relaxed against his chest, loving the warmth of his touch. I felt him kiss the top of my head, making my scalp tingle, and then pull me tighter. It'll be all right, I thought. Even if I get sent to Saint Anne's, I'll still have Hunter.

After another moment he pulled away. "There's been some news," he said.

I felt my stomach tighten. "Your father?" I breathed.

Hunter smiled wryly. "No," he said. "Yours. Apparently Ciaran has been very active since his arrival in Madrid. That sigil you placed on him shows that he's visited a few of the top people on the council's watch list. Of course, there isn't any concrete proof—yet—that he has been the one behind the attacks against you. But one of the people he visited is Lenore Ammett, a witch known to have very strong telekinetic powers, who is suspected of abusing them." He paused, watching as the meaning of his words sank in. He nodded slightly and went on. "If she's helping him, he may have found a way to get around the proximity problem. Based on what we know, Ciaran looks to be the guilty party. Erin thinks so. The council thinks so." Hunter's jaw set into a firm line. "And I think so."

The words were both comforting and unsettling. Of course I wanted Ciaran to be stopped. But then again . . . he was my father.

"So how are they going to stop him?" I asked.

"With our help," Hunter replied.

"Ours?" I repeated faintly.

Hunter nodded. "All of ours. Morgan, I know you're grounded, but this situation has become very grave. Erin has found a spell that she thinks can help us. It's a deflection spell—when it is used against a witch, any magick that he works will come back to him threefold."

I frowned. "Isn't that just the threefold law?" I asked.

"No." Wind ruffled an errant strand of Hunter's pale hair, and I brushed it away from his face. "The threefold law is simply a general rule of the magickal universe, like karma, or what goes around comes around, as you Americans say." He grinned. "But the universe can take a long time to set things right."

"But the deflection spell?" I prompted.

"Works immediately." Hunter's green eyes glittered. "And harshly."

"Wait—why doesn't the council just use this all the time to punish anyone who's abusing their powers?" I asked, thinking of Selene, who almost succeeded in killing me—and probably did succeed in killing others—before she was brought to justice.

"The spell has some drawbacks," Hunter admitted slowly.

"Such as?"

Hunter cleared his throat. "Well," he said, "the spell requires a great deal of combined magick to work. And it tends to sap the energy of those who use it. Basically once the spell is finished, everyone in our circle will be the way you are now—possibly worse—"

"Which means that if someone else is behind these incidents or if someone else, like one of the other Amyranth branches, decides to attack us, we'll be in serious trouble," I finished for him.

"Yes," Hunter said. "But on the positive side, the spell may not sap our energy for that long. We'll probably just feel ill for about a day. Erin is fairly certain—"

"Erin is *fairly* certain?" I repeated. "Erin hasn't done this spell before?"

"No one in the council has," Hunter admitted uncomfortably. "It's strictly forbidden because of the dangers involved. Also because of the source. But Erin has managed to convince the council that this is one time it's worth the risk."

"What source?" I asked. "Where's the spell from?"

"It's from a book by Harris Stoughton," Hunter replied. "Apparently Alyce gave it to Erin the other day."

"I was there," I said faintly, trying to suppress the shudder that had run through my body at the mention of Harris Stoughton's name. I was liking this plan less and less. "You think this is a good idea?"

Hunter shrugged. "We haven't heard much about Amyranth lately. I went to New York City yesterday and did some digging—it seems that none of the other members of that cell could have been behind this. They all seem to be lying low. And if we do use the spell, we'll know right away whether it worked. First, we'll feel the effects. Second, the spell will hit Ciaran hard—probably making him physically ill for at least a few days. That ought to make it easier for one of the Seekers in Spain to apprehend him. This is our chance to help out."

I looked at Hunter, feeling his desire to stop Ciaran almost like it was my own. I knew that he wanted to bring Ciaran in for my safety, but there was something else behind it as well. Hunter was a Seeker by nature, not just by training. It was what he lived for. It was a side of him that frightened me. It was also part of the reason I loved him.

"What do you need me to do?" I asked.

"Erin wants to hold a circle tonight: you, me, Sky, and Alyce. I know you're grounded, but do you think there's any way you can make it?"

I shook my head. "No. My parents are really upset. They want—" I looked up at the redbrick school building, which contained all of the friends and classmates that I'd hung out with my entire life. "They want to transfer me to Saint Anne's."

Hunter frowned. "The Catholic school? They decided?"

I nodded. "You know they don't approve of Wicca."

Hunter sighed. "I'll help you get through this."

"They feel like I'm slipping away from them." I shrugged. "I guess I have been, in a way. Anyway, trust me, there's no way I can make it to a circle tonight."

"Right." Hunter looked disappointed, if not surprised. "Well, we really need you, Morgan. So I've brought you this." He reached into his pocket and pulled out a small dark blue stone. A vein of white ran through it, and it reminded me of the night sky lit up by the Milky Way.

"What is it?" I asked, taking the stone from him.

"It's lapis lazuli," Hunter explained. "It facilitates understanding and communication. I've strengthened it with a spell. If you place this stone on your forehead, I ought to be able to send you thoughts and images, and you ought to be able to do the same to me, like a witch message, only better. It will be almost as if you were there at the circle with us. I should be able to channel your energy. Even with your power reined, the spell and my magick ought to allow the two of us to communicate. But once your power has been unreined, you'll be able to participate fully."

My heart skipped about five beats. "You're unreining my power?"

"Of course," Hunter replied. "Erin feels terrible that you were ever reined in the first place. Clearly you had nothing to do with what was happening."

I slipped my arms around his neck and gave him a kiss. "Thank you," I said.

"There's nothing to thank me for."

My lips were still warm where they had touched Hunter's. I wanted to contradict him, but I didn't. Instead I asked, "Has there been any new word from your parents?"

Hunter pressed his lips together. "No," he replied. "But I haven't given up. I've thought about the clues I've had—a walled city, the fact that I spoke in French. There are a number of walled medieval cities in France. I've asked the council whether I can have leave to go look for my father and mother—"

My heart literally—literally—stopped beating for a moment.

"—but they've refused. They think my evidence isn't strong enough. They won't tell me what research they've done so far, and they won't send someone to France now. But it looks like there might be someone who is willing to search *for* me. Someone who isn't in the council and isn't bound by their rules."

I was so relieved that Hunter wasn't leaving that the ominous note in his voice barely registered in my mind. "Who?" I asked.

"Sky."

"What?" I asked. Sky was going to France? What about Kithic? "How long will she be gone?"

Hunter looked sad. "It's unclear. She's quit her job already. After she's finished in France, she may go back to England," he explained.

"But—but—" I sputtered. Sky and I had never been terribly close. Still, I didn't want her to leave. Hunter reached out and touched the tips of my long hair.

"We'll all miss her," he said. "But she doesn't want to stay here, Morgan. Things have been hard for her." Hunter looked at me, and I knew that he was talking about Sky's breakup with Raven. I knew she had to be excited at the thought of going home to her friends. "Besides," Hunter added, "I need her help."

I nodded. Hunter was right—this was important. I knew that even though he wasn't saying it, Hunter's didn't want to send her. He wanted to go himself.

By the time I stepped into the school building, the bell ending first period had already rung. This was actually a good thing. If I had walked inside in the middle of first period, I would have almost certainly been stopped by Assistant Principal Collello, who seemed to think that it was his personal duty to hand out detentions to as many students as possible. But by coming in during the minutes between first and second period, I could just blend in with all the other students and make my way to class.

I pulled off my cap and felt static running through my hair. It was probably standing on end. I decided I'd better make a quick stop at the girls' room to check if I was presentable before wandering into class. I didn't want to look like I was just coming in from outside, after all.

A quick glance in the mirror showed me that the problem was more serious than I'd thought. My hair looked like a fright wig. I raked my fingers through it. It didn't help. I was just concluding that the situation was hopeless when the door swung open and Bree walked in.

"Morgan," she said quickly. "I'm glad you're here. I've been looking everywhere." She leaned gracefully against the sink and swung her backpack from her shoulder, balancing it on the shelf in front of us.

"I was way late." I wet my fingers under the faucet and attempted to comb my hair with them again.

"Do you want a brush?" Bree asked, rummaging around in her leather backpack. She finally pulled out a wide-toothed comb.

"Fantastic," I said taking it from her. I pulled it through my hair, which began to settle down. Thank goodness.

"Listen, Morgan, I need to talk to you."

Our eyes met in the mirror. "What's going on?" I asked.

"Well, Robbie and I finally talked. He told me that he'd spoken to you and that he thought there had been a big misunderstanding."

"That's great!" I said. "So are you guys back together?"

"Well, yes," Bree admitted. She twirled the ends of her hair. The worried gesture.

I frowned. "So what's wrong?" I asked.

Bree looked at herself in the mirror, then looked back at me. "It's just that—when I thought that Robbie and I were breaking up, I sort of . . ."

My stomach dropped. "What?" I demanded. "What did you do?"

"I sort of . . . fooled around with Matt."

"Oh my God." I wheeled to face her. "Did you—"

"No." Bree folded her arms across her chest. "Absolutely not. Just, you know, kissing."

I couldn't believe this. Matt Adler! My mind flashed back to the day I saw him cheating on Jenna with Raven. I felt ill. "And you didn't tell Robbie?"

"I didn't know how to." Bree's voice was pleading. "I mean, it isn't exactly cheating because I thought we were broken up. It was really just a mistake. One that will *not* happen again. But I got scared that Robbie might not take it that way. So I kept my mouth shut."

I looked at her closely, trying to remain calm. I knew from personal experience with Mary K. that keeping the truth quiet was usually a mistake. "Keeping your mouth shut about this is like lying, Bree," I told her. "It's the same thing."

Bree bit her lip. I knew that wasn't what she'd wanted to hear.

"So you're going to talk to him?" I prompted.

Bree hesitated. "I guess so."

I folded my arms across my chest. "You might want to do it soon—like before Matt tells anyone that he made out with you."

Bree's face went white. "He wouldn't."

I shrugged. "He didn't think you were cheating, either, right? So he has no reason to keep quiet about it. And I'm guessing he'll boast."

That seemed to do it. Bree thought for a moment, then nodded. "Okay," she said finally. "Okay." I handed her the brush, and she stuck it in her bag. "Did you hear about Sky?" she asked.

"Just now."

"I can't believe it," Bree said. "What's Kithic going to be like? I just can't imagine circles without her." She shook her head and sighed.

"Me either."

"I don't know, Morgan," Bree murmured. "Sometimes I feel like everything's falling apart."

I thought of Hunter, my father, my reined power, my family. . . . I considered telling Bree about my parents' wanting to send me to Saint Anne's but decided that could wait. She had enough to worry about. "Yeah," I answered instead. "I know what you mean."

12.
Restoration

October 4, 1971

I can feel the darkness closing in.

Today, the day after my argument with Mother, I went back to the library and pulled out The Book. I don't know what made me do it—I suppose I thought that it might have some advice on how to stop the same dark magick it unleashed. Which it did. Page after page on binding witches, both in secret and in the open. It even had a section on how to bind one's own magick. But I wasn't sure—I mean, I didn't know for sure that Sam was behind the latest piece of dark magick.

I decided to look for another option.

I flipped through the book, skimming it, and finally came across a chapter called "On the Movements of Objectes Through the Aire." Just like the plates and the drawer in the kitchen, I thought, and the lamp in the corner. So I read it. And guess what it said? It said that some witches, when they're in an agitated state of mind, can mentally move objects without realizing it.

So Sam could be behind these events, I realized. He wouldn't have to be into dark magick to be behind them. As long as he is nearby and is familiar with the objects in question, he could move them with his mind. Obviously he's eaten off the plates in the kitchen often enough to be able to picture them. And he was in the house both times.

I went to leave the library. But as I stood there redrawing the sigils of protection and obscurity around the door, I suddenly realized something.

Sam doesn't know about the library.

He won't be shown the library until his initiation. He doesn't even know it exists. So how could he have made the lamp fall over inside it?

In fact, there's only one witch in the house who knows about the library and is in an agitated state of mind. The same person who was present at both events. The one person I would never suspect.

Me.

—Sarah Curtis

"With this salt, I purify my circle." I couldn't wait to be unbound. I sprinkled salt around the large circle I had drawn lightly on the floor of my room. It was midnight, and my family was asleep. Still, I had shoved a chair up against the door leading from my room into the bathroom and a few books up against the main door to my room. I didn't want any more people accidentally barging into my room while I was in the middle of making magick.

I picked up the lapis lazuli from where I had placed it at the center of the circle. The stone felt cool in my hand. The gentle silk of my birth mother's green robe felt smooth against my skin, and even though my power was still reined, these two things made me feel like I was surrounded by good magick.

Lying down in the center of the circle, I placed the smooth stone on my forehead. I wasn't exactly sure what to do, so I decided to try casting out my senses.

I could feel Hunter's presence almost like he was in the room with me. My eyes were filled with fog that slowly began to lift slightly. As I looked around me, I saw that I was no longer in my room. I was in Hunter's living room. Sitting across from me was Alyce. To her right was Sky; to her left was Erin. Sky's lips were moving, but I couldn't hear what she was saying. Soon the others closed their eyes, and I saw their lips moving as well. They were chanting, I guessed. I watched all of this through a thin film of haze, like static from a channel that wasn't coming in clearly. What was this spell they were casting? It looked totally unfamiliar to me.

After a few moments Erin lit a black pillar candle. Then Alyce drew out a long string of thread and burned it over the candle so that it was broken in two. Silver flame licked up the thread, which dissolved into a fine, shimmery powder. Alyce blew on the powder so that it floated through the room, growing into a large cloud of sparkling dust. Soon everyone was covered in it. The powder gave everything it landed on a magickal glow, as if the room were bathed in the rosy light of a sunrise. All the while their lips were moving in the chant. It was eerie, like watching a suspense movie with the sound turned off, but somehow beautiful.

Erin placed her fingers in a bowl of water, then passed her hand over it three times. Quite suddenly the haze began to lift, and I could see everyone clearly. At the same time I realized that for the first time in days, I didn't have a headache. In fact, I felt wonderful, as if I'd just taken a long nap and a hot shower. I noticed that I was very, very hungry. That was when I knew that the ceremony I had just witnessed had restored my magick.

"Hunter," Sky said to me. Her voice was far away, like a voice in a dream. "Hunter, is she with us?"

"Yes," I said to Sky. I had spoken with Hunter's voice, almost as if we were one person, one will. It was then that I fully understood that I was seeing through his eyes—that I was actually *within* Hunter. I wasn't even certain whether the intention to speak had been my own or his. In the next moment I felt a rush of excitement. It was a visceral feeling, almost like lust, and once again I wasn't sure whether the feelings were Hunter's or my own. Suddenly I felt very self-conscious.

"Welcome to the circle, Morgan," Erin said.

There was so much I wanted to say—I wanted everyone to know how grateful I was to have my magick back; I wanted Sky to know that I was sorry she was leaving. But the power of the moment was intense, and it seemed inappropriate to address anything but the grim task at hand. I focused my energy on Hunter's presence. I felt a warm rush of strength and love and somehow knew that Hunter was sending me his emotions. I pulled those feelings around me like a blanket.

Erin pulled the book, still wrapped in its dark shroud, from its place beside her and placed it in her lap. After untying the silk cover, she turned to a page she had marked with a red bookmark. Erin closed her eyes for a moment and seemed to take a deep breath to steady herself. Then she opened her eyes and began to read the spell aloud.

The words were harsh and ugly, half of them written in an ancient language that I didn't understand—one that seemed older than any language I'd heard before. They seemed to force their way out of Erin's throat, as if she could hardly bear to utter them. Alyce's eyes were closed, and she was grimacing as if in pain with every word Erin spoke. Sweat broke out on Sky's forehead, and a bead trickled down the side of her face. Even I felt dizzy and tired, although I couldn't tell whether it was the effect of the spell or the strain of experiencing the circle through Hunter. I felt a current run through me like a bolt of electricity, and I knew it was the power of the circle growing and combining, running through all of us.

I felt a wave of exhaustion—Hunter's, I was almost certain. Alyce's face was flushing pink, then darker red. Her grimace grew wider, and it seemed like she could hardly bear what was happening. Tendrils of her gray hair worked their way loose from her long braid. I noticed this in a moment, a period of time shorter than a heartbeat, then slowly, slowly, the haze began to return. The scene was filling with fog that grew thicker with each passing moment. *What's happening?* I thought frantically, but not fast enough. The words beat back against me as if I was shouting into the wind. I felt certain that they had reached no one—not even Hunter.

I became aware of a sound, a sound very much like the

roaring ocean beating against the rocks, then drawing back, then beating once again against the rocks. It was a sound I knew, though it took me a moment to place it.

It was the sound of my breathing.

I opened my eyes and found myself in my own room. I tried to cast out my senses again for Hunter but found that I couldn't. Hunter, Sky, Alyce, and Erin—had their magick been sapped, too? Did that mean the spell had been successful? I had no idea—I hoped so.

I couldn't believe that everything had happened so quickly. I struggled to sit up, and the lapis lazuli fell from my forehead with a thunk against the floor. I picked it up and held it against my lips for a moment.

I felt like hell.

Standing up, I pulled off Maeve's robe and folded it carefully. Then I yanked on a flannel nightgown and crept to the hiding place where I kept all of my mother's tools, behind the HVAC vent, and carefully put the robe back in its place. I set the lapis lazuli on my nightstand. Crawling into bed, I gently lifted Dagda's soft form and placed him at the end of the bed. I stroked his fur, then pulled the covers over me.

Staring into the darkness, I wished I could call Hunter . . . just to hear his voice and to know whether the spell had worked. It seemed cruel to have my magick back—to feel it flowing through me so fiercely for a few moments—and then to have it ripped away again. Still, I knew the magick would return. And I knew that Hunter would, too.

And if there was one thing I had learned how to do lately, it was wait.

*   *   *

I expected to feel better when I woke up the next morning, which is why it was such a rude shock when I still felt horrible. Every muscle ached, and when I tried to sit up, my body actually shook with the effort. Still, I forced myself over to my dresser and pulled on some fresh clothes. I had to go to school today—my history paper was due. I'd spent practically every spare moment, every lunch period and study hall, working on it. Even if it wouldn't help my quest to stay out of Catholic school, I wasn't about to let those precious twenty points of extra credit go without a fight.

I thought I'd never make it to fifth period. But when I walked into history class and placed my paper on Mr. Powell's desk, I felt proud of myself and happy. Even though my parents had never approved of my topic, the paper was good, and I knew it.

After school I came home and fell straight into bed. I didn't wake up until eight o'clock, when my mom appeared in my bedroom with a tray, looking worried. "Are you all right, Morgan?" she asked.

"Fine," I said, my voice thick from sleep. "I just stayed up late last night. I had to hand in my history paper today." Both of these things were true, although unrelated.

My mom nodded. "I made you some soup." She placed the tray on the floor by my bed. "Lean forward."

I obeyed, and she plumped up the pillows behind me. Then she placed the tray on my lap. The soup was minestrone—one of my favorites. "Delicious," I said when I'd had a spoonful.

"I didn't wake you because I figured you needed your

rest," my mom said. "Besides, Dad and I like to have a romantic dinner alone sometimes."

"Where's Mary K.?" I asked.

"She's over at Alisa's house." Mom traced a finger over the edge of my afghan. "Apparently Alisa was out sick today. Mary K. went over to give her the Spanish assignment." My mother studied the pattern in the blanket carefully. I knew she was holding something back. Almost as if she felt me looking at her, my mom leaned over and brushed my hair away from my face.

"I really don't feel sick," I assured her. "I was just tired. I feel better already."

I think my mom could tell I was lying, but she didn't press me. Instead she just stood up. "Leave the tray by your bed when you're finished," she instructed. "I'll come back and get it later."

"Thanks, Mom," I said.

She nodded and closed the door behind her as she left. I had another spoonful of soup and realized that I really did feel better—a little better, anyway. For once my mom and I hadn't argued about grades, or beliefs, or Catholic school. It had seemed, for a moment, almost like we were back to normal.

Almost.

13.
Flame

I can't write much—The pen feels like lead in my hand.

This morning I woke up feeling so sick That my sheets were actually hurting me. When Dad Took my Temperature, he flipped out—iT was 103 degrees. He gave me some Tylenol and made me drink some juice, Then Took me To Dr. Hawthorne's office. He Took my blood and a strep culture. But he didn't really have any idea what was making me so sick. He seemed worried That my Temperature had spiked so quickly but couldn't explain iT. He says iT's The flu. DocTors always say iT's The flu.

Mary K. came over for a while, which made me feel a biT betTer, but now I'm feeling worse again—feverish and nauseated. NoThing seems To help.

I'm scared. I wish I could call someone in KiThic. I miss iT so much That I'm starTing To Think I made a mistake by leaving The coven. But I guess iT's Too late To go back now.

—Alisa

By the time I stumbled downstairs and into the kitchen on Saturday morning, Mary K. was already dressed and stacking the breakfast dishes in the dishwasher.

"Is Alisa there?" Mary K. asked, and I realized she was talking into the cordless as she straightened up and closed the dishwasher. "She is?" There was a long pause. "What's wrong?" An even longer pause. "Oh. Okay." Mary K. reached out and gripped the countertop. "Can she have visitors?" she asked. "Well, thanks, Mr. Soto," she said finally. "Tell her . . . tell her I hope she gets better soon." Mary K.'s eyebrows drew together in a worried frown as she clicked off the phone and placed it on the counter.

I was tempted to sneak away—this was none of my business—but Mary K.'s expression disturbed me. I cleared my throat to let her know I was there and asked, "Everything okay?"

Mary K. turned to face me. Her eyebrows lifted, and for a moment I thought she was going to yell at me for eavesdropping, but she seemed to change her mind. "Alisa's really sick," she said finally. "She's in the hospital."

"Oh," I said. A feeling of dread squeezed my lungs. "What's wrong?"

Mary K.'s voice shook a little. "Nobody knows. All they know is that it's serious. She's . . . she's not even conscious. Her dad is really freaked out."

"Oh my God, Mary K." I went over to her and hugged her. "That's horrible."

Mary K. started to cry. I didn't say anything . . . I just rubbed her back the way I used to do when we were children. After a few moments she took a couple of shaky breaths. "It's just scary," she whispered into my shoulder.

"I know," I replied. "But she's in the hospital now. The doctors are there—they'll figure out what's wrong with her." I rubbed her back again. "It's going to be okay." I hoped it was true.

Mary K. pulled away from me. "Morgan," she said, and stopped.

"What?" I asked.

"Morgan, I'm sorry I told Mom and Dad about your friend."

It took a minute for me to figure out who she was talking about. "You mean Erin?" I asked.

"I was just so s-s-scared." Another tear squeezed out of the corner of Mary K.'s eye and trickled down the side of her cheek. I brushed it away.

"I know," I said. "It's okay."

We looked at each other a moment. "I don't want anything to happen," Mary K. said.

"It won't," I assured her.

"How do you know?" she demanded. "I mean—why are you risking it?"

I sighed. "Mary K., magick isn't just horrible, dangerous, dark things. It can also be beautiful and wonderful. It's part of who I am. And I'm—" How could I put it? "—I'm strong. You don't have to worry about me. I can take care of myself." The words were more forceful than I really believed, but saying them actually made me feel better.

They seemed to have the same effect on Mary K. She straightened up and passed her hands over her face, then she tucked her hair behind her ears. "Morgan—would you take me to see Alisa?"

"Of course," I said quickly. I was about to ask whether she wanted to go right now, but then I remembered. "Oh, crap, I'm grounded. We'll have to ask Mom and Dad if it's okay."

"They're out running errands," Mary K. said, "and visiting hours are only until three."

"Can we go tomorrow?"

Mary K. nodded. "Sure. That would be great." She started to head out of the room, then turned back. "Thanks, Morgan," she said.

I nodded. "No problem."

Mary K. smiled at me, and for a moment she looked just like the sister I knew—the one who loved me, no matter what.

That night I moped around the house for a couple of hours. The house was deserted—Mom and Dad were over at the Berkows' for dinner, and Mary K. had gone over to her friend Susan's house. My parents had given me permission to watch television, but there was nothing decent on any of the channels. My chest ached. I still felt awful from the previous night's spell, but more than that, I was sad about tonight's circle. It would be the last one with Sky, and I was missing it.

What I needed was magick, and if I couldn't go to Sharon's house along with the rest of Kithic, I could at least try to scry by myself. Maybe some of my power had returned.

Up in my room, the match hissed and flared as I lit my pillar candle. I breathed deeply and stared into the flame. I could feel the rays of warmth radiating off the candle. The heat sank into me, driving away the cold draft in my room. As my breathing grew more regular, I felt calm . . . and after a while, happy. I looked into the depths of the small blaze. The graduated colors, the blue, orange, and yellow, of the fire seemed to swirl together and grow. They flared and changed color, first to red, then purple, then violet, then green. The green fire twirled slowly, like an eddy in the ocean, and I realized that the fire was showing me something and bent closer.

In the depths of the green flame I saw a figure—Hunter. He was waving at me, but it wasn't a wave that beckoned me closer. It was more like a farewell. My heart quickened, but the image faded. I was left only with the swirling green flame, the color of Hunter's eyes. Slowly it faded to violet, then purple, then red . . . and in a moment it was an ordinary candle flame again.

What did it mean? Was it a portent—an image of the future? Or was it a picture of something that *might* come to pass but might not? I didn't know. I was afraid to know.

Although I tried to comfort myself with the certain knowledge that my power was back, I couldn't stop the feeling of dread that squeezed my lungs in its grip, making it difficult to breathe. Hunter and I had been through so much together, and I'd been so happy that he was near me, safe.

I had a horrible feeling that everything was about to change.

I took a long hot shower and put on a clean nightgown. Dagda hobbled into my room and sniffed at a pile of books in the corner. I patted my bed, and he leapt up onto it, purring as I stroked him. It was late—almost midnight—and I was about to click off the lamp by the side of my bed when my eye fell on a flash of midnight blue on my nightstand. It was the piece of lapis lazuli. I picked it up and rubbed it .

I could call Hunter, I realized. If my magick was back, then his must be, too.

I lay back on my bed and placed the lapis on my forehead, closing my eyes and forming a mental image of Hunter. *I am here,* I thought. *Hunter, I am here.*

Morgan.

It was both a voice and not a voice—almost like my own thought, yet somehow separate—and I knew that it was Hunter.

I miss you, I thought.

Yes, he replied. *I feel the same.*

I couldn't exactly see anything—just the same sort of grainy darkness that I always saw when I closed my eyes. But after a few moments the darkness seemed to grow lighter. It continued to pale until it was almost the same purple-gray as twilight—or as the sky before the sun rises.

Kithic? I thought. *How was the circle?*

Melancholy. Hunter's word reverberated through my mind. *Sky is sad to be leaving tomorrow, although she doesn't say so. And of course, Alisa has left us. Everyone was gloomy. You should be glad that you weren't there.*

I wish I had been there. As it is, I won't get to say good-bye.

Hunter's thoughts were gentle. *Sky understands.*

The darkness before my eyes grew even lighter—pinkish, like the inside of a conch shell. With the next breath I took, I had the sense that Hunter was in my room. His distinct odor of soap and clean laundry filled my nostrils. Still, I knew that he was in another house, halfway across town.

I feel like you're here with me. The words were Hunter's. I wondered if he was experiencing the same thing I was.

The spell, I asked, *did it work?*

According to the council, Ciaran hasn't moved for twenty-four hours, Hunter replied. *A Seeker will move in on him tomorrow.*

And then there's the matter of our magick. Mine completely disappeared Thursday night. . . . This is the first glimmer I've of it all day.

It feels wonderful. The words drifted through my mind, sending chills through my body. I wasn't sure whether they were mine or Hunter's. But it didn't matter.

At the center of the pinkish void, a small ball of silvery flame flared and began to pulse. It flared brilliantly until the entire space was lit with dazzling whiteness. It warmed me, as if I were standing with my face to the sun.

You are so brave. The words, the words, mine or his? *I love you.*

I didn't send any more thoughts. It seemed unnecessary. Hunter's presence was all I had wanted . . . and now I felt like I was surrounded by it, almost engulfed by it.

I knew what this light was. It wasn't Hunter's energy or mine. It was something beyond the two of us—something greater than the sum of two halves. This light was the energy between us, the power of mùirn beatha dàns, soul mates.

14.
Heal

October 5, 1971

   I tried to talk to Sam about what's been happening, but I never got the chance. The minute I mentioned the Harris Stoughton book, he became <u>furious</u>. He demanded to know whether I had destroyed it, and when I said I hadn't, he started shouting.

   I was already on edge, and having him yell at me set me off. I told him that he should have burned the book himself. He was the one who stole it, he was the one who brought it home, he was the one who tried one of its spells even <u>after</u> I told him the book was evil. I was sick of trying to help him! As we stood there screaming at each other, I was suddenly struck with a splitting headache, a piercing, stabbing pain.

   Sam threw up his hands and stormed out of my room. I followed him, still yelling—and so I saw what happened. As he reached the top of the stairs, the mahogany table in the hall gave a violent lurch. It slid as if the entire house had tipped on its foundation and slammed into him.

"Sam!" I screamed.

Sam clawed at the banister, but he couldn't stop himself from falling. He tumbled down the entire stair, head over heels. When he reached the bottom, he lay perfectly still for a moment, his leg twisted behind him. He looked up at me for one moment, then turned his head to the side and vomited.

"Sam!" I screamed again, then ran to call an ambulance. I knelt beside him while we waited for it to arrive, but he didn't open his eyes again. I felt numb as I rode in back with him to the local hospital. Luckily the doctors say that he's only got a broken leg and a mild concussion. He'll be all right. With a fall like his, they said, things could have been much worse.

Much worse—if things had been much worse, he'd be _dead_.

This can't go on. I know what happened with the table—I did it. I did it, and I can never do anything like that again.

I won't let another person die because of the Curtis witchcraft.

—Sarah Curtis

I woke up feeling fully rested. My body no longer felt achy or tired—I hadn't felt so alive in what seemed like weeks. I glanced at the clock, expecting it to read somewhere close to noon.

7:30 A.M.

Just then I heard the gentle hiss of the shower, and I knew my sister was stepping into it. It was early Sunday morning. The pale light was just beginning to peek through my curtains. I could sleep as long as I wanted. Sighing happily, I lay back against my pillows and closed my eyes.

Then I opened them again. I was wide awake.

I thought about the night before—the beautiful, magickal way I'd been able to experience being with Hunter. It had felt so wonderful to have him with me that I would have thought the whole experience had been a dream, if it hadn't seemed so real. Beyond real—almost *more* than real, if such a thing was possible.

Mary K.'s shower ended. I waited a few minutes, but she didn't come into my room to wake me up for church. I thought of the smile she'd given me the night before.

I heard the familiar sound of my father's slippers as he padded down the stairs into the kitchen. There, then, was another thing I had missed—my family.

I threw off my covers and walked over to my closet. I pulled out a gray flannel skirt and a red sweater. Quickly I pulled on my clothes and brushed my hair.

I was going to church.

"Hi," I said as I walked into the kitchen.

My mother looked up from the paper she was reading. "Morgan," she said, her eyebrows lifted in surprise. She took in my outfit from head to toe, then smiled. "You look very nice," she said.

I grabbed a Diet Coke from the refrigerator. "I thought I'd come with you to church this morning."

My dad stared at me from where he was standing by the sink, his coffee cup lifted halfway to his mouth. He set it down on the counter. "Well, well." A pleased grin spread across his face. Looking down at his bathrobe, he said, "I guess I'm lagging behind."

Dad took his coffee and headed upstairs just as Mary K. came down. "What are you wearing?" she asked, staring at me.

"Morgan is coming to church with us this morning," Mom said, as if it was the most obvious and normal thing in the world.

"Oh," Mary K. said. Apparently this possibility hadn't occurred to her. "Great!" She grinned at me and went to the refrigerator. "You want toast?" she asked.

The normalcy of the question seemed like something from another time. "Sounds good," I said, sitting down at the table. In fact, it sounded better than good. It sounded like the best thing in the whole world.

Stepping into the church was like visiting an old friend, welcoming and familiar. There was the spicy smell of the incense our church uses and the odor of faded roses as I passed by Mrs. Beacon's pew. The strains of organ music drifted over the congregation. Mom's friend, Mrs. Lu, turned and gave me a big smile as we slipped into the pew behind hers. I smiled back and waved to her three-year-old daughter, Nellie, who giggled.

When it came time to take communion, I leaned over to my mom and said, "I think I'm going to skip this." I just didn't feel right about it—somehow taking communion seemed like

a definite commitment to Catholicism. Even though I appreci-
ated the beauty of the service, I wasn't about to stop practicing Wicca. I was glad that my family loved coming here, and I
loved it, too—but Wicca had chosen me as much as I had
chosen it, and I wanted to find a way to keep both of my reli-
gions in my life.

I half expected my mom to frown or look disapproving,
but she just squeezed my knee and followed my sister and
father to the front of the church. A short while later the
service was over.

A new level of calm swept over me as my family and I
stepped outside. The sky was a clear blue, and a few small
clouds tumbled across it. I was glad I had come.

"Mom, Dad," Mary K. said as we walked to the car.
"Would it be okay if Morgan took me to the hospital to see
Alisa later?"

My mom looked sideways at my dad, who nodded.
Parental telepathy. "I guess it's all right," my mom said.

I smiled at my mom, and she smiled back. Of course, she
would never refuse to allow Mary K. to see a friend in the
hospital, but she could have insisted on taking Mary K. there
herself. I felt like she was finally beginning to see how hard
I'd been trying.

"Thanks," Mary K. said. But she wasn't looking at my
parents. She was looking at me.

My boots clattered as we walked down the long corridor
in the hospital toward Alisa's room. The hospital was quiet,
and I found it kind of unnerving. Mary K. had seemed really
eager to leave right away once we got home, so I didn't

bother changing, and now I felt overdressed and awkward. Every step I took made me sound like a lumbering elephant.

Mary K. looked down at the small red-and-white teddy bear she was clutching against her chest. She had insisted that we stop at the drugstore before we came so that she could pick up a card for Alisa, and the teddy bears had been on sale. Bringing the bear was the kind of thing Mary K. was really good at—the kind of thing I never would have thought to do. "It's so weird," Mary K. said as she checked the door numbers. The nurse had told us that we'd find Alisa in room 341. "We've been in two hospitals this week."

Personally, I thought that the animal hospital was more comfortable and homey than this sterile, silent place, but I didn't say so.

"I'm glad Dagda's okay," Mary K. went on. "I hope Alisa will be, too."

"She will," I said. My voice conveyed much more certainty than I felt.

Mary K. gave me a sideways look but didn't reply. I wondered what she was thinking. I had no idea whether she knew how close to death Dagda had been. Did she realize that Erin had healed him?

"Three forty-one," Mary K. announced as we walked up to a door at the end of the hallway. It was half open. There was no noise coming from inside except for the steady beeps and whirring of machinery.

My sister looked at me uncertainly, and I realized that she was frightened. "It's okay," I told her, and rapped lightly on the door. There was no response, so I pushed it open a little farther. "Hello?" I called softly, but there was no reply. I was secretly relieved. The last thing I felt like doing was making polite conversation with Alisa's family. I nodded at my sister and stepped inside. Mary K. followed me.

Alisa's bed was at the far end of the dim room, near windows that were shrouded in curtains. She was either asleep or unconscious, and Mary K. sucked in her breath when she saw the machines clustered around her. Alisa's hair was limp on the pillow, and below her closed eyelashes were dark circles. Her cheeks were sunken and pale, her lips chapped and peeling.

How could someone get so sick so quickly?

Mary K. hesitated, then placed the teddy bear on the small table next to Alisa's bed, propping the card up against it. "So that she'll see it when she wakes up," she whispered to me.

"Do you want to wait a while?" I asked.

Mary K. nodded. "If you don't mind," she said.

"Sure," I said, looking back at Alisa. I could only glance at her for a few seconds before I had to turn away. She looked horrible.

There was a yellow chair next to the side table, which I lowered myself into. In spite of its hideous color, it was big and comfortable. I patted the empty space next to me— there was more than enough room for Mary K. to fit. "Do you want to sit?"

"Yeah . . ." Mary K. was staring at Alisa, not moving. She seemed to be in her own world, pondering something. Suddenly she turned to me. "I'm going to get a Coke," she said. "I saw a machine in the front hall. Do you want anything? A Diet Coke?"

There was a strange edge in her tone, as if she were nervous. I wondered whether she was upset about the way

Alisa looked—she certainly was a pitiful sight. "Are you okay?" I asked. "We don't have to stay here if you don't want to."

"No, no," Mary K. insisted. "I want to. I just . . . want a Coke."

I frowned at her. Her tone was strange and tense, as if she wanted to tell me more than she was saying. But—what? "Do you want me to come with you?" I asked.

"No—that's okay. I'll be right back. I mean," she said quickly as she raked a hand through her hair, "I mean I'll be back in a few minutes. The soda machine is near the entrance. It'll take me a few minutes to get back." Mary K. glanced at Alisa, then at me, and in that one glance I understood.

Mary K. wanted to leave me alone with Alisa.

She thought I could heal her.

Before I could even protest, Mary K. was out the door. Her footsteps retreated down the hall, first quickly, then more slowly. I guessed that she remembered she needed to take her time to get the soda.

I glanced at Alisa and had to suppress a shudder. She was so very sick. And I wasn't even the one who had healed Dagda—Erin had done that! I knew next to nothing about healing, even with Alyce's knowledge inside me. I wished Erin were there with me. I didn't know whether she could heal Alisa, either, but she sure as hell knew a lot more about it than I did.

I sat on my hands, swallowing the sob that was rising in my throat. But what if I can help her? I wondered. How can I sit here and do nothing when Alisa might be—

Don't think it, I commanded myself.

—dying. The word stung my consciousness like a fresh burn. I pictured Mary K.'s face. I tried to imagine what I would tell her. You see, Mary K., I know enough magick to fight dark forces, but not enough to help your best friend. . . . My vision blurred, and I rubbed my chest where it had begun to ache.

Alisa drew in a ragged, shuddering breath, then moaned. My stomach dropped. "Please don't," I whispered. Alisa grew quiet, but that didn't make me feel better. I had to do something to help her. Even if I couldn't heal her, maybe I could do a spell to take away some of the pain. Quickly I reached out and took her hand.

Immediately the cool, steady pulse of the heart rate monitor began a high-pitched scream. I dropped Alisa's hand and jumped back, my heart pumping wildly. What had I done? I hadn't even touched the machines! Without thinking, I screamed, "Mary K.! Mary K.!" I should have called for a doctor, but I didn't even think of it.

The door was flung open and a tall African American nurse exploded into the room, pushing a cart full of machinery. "You're going to have to get out of here," she said to me as a doctor hurried in behind her and rushed to check Alisa's monitors.

A chill breeze blew over me—I felt like the temperature in the room had dropped forty degrees. Goddess, help me! I thought. Alisa's body shook with convulsions.

Mary K. appeared in the doorway, looking tense and pale. "What happened?" Her wide eyes fastened on Alisa's machines, which were still going crazy. "Oh my God—what *happened?*" She stared at Alisa in horror.

I steered her out the door. "I don't know," I said as Mary K. tried to peer past me. Another nurse ran down the hall and pushed past us into Alisa's room. "Look, the nurse said we should get out of here," I said as calmly as I could, fighting my panic. Every nerve in my body was screaming.

"But we can't just leave," Mary K. protested. Her eyes were filled with tears.

"We're in the way," I said. "Mary K.—I'm sorry."

I was. I was so sorry. But I didn't know what to say. I had barely touched Alisa's hand, and I hadn't even been using magick at all.

Something had happened—but what? And why? I couldn't have caused that, I told myself. I didn't even do anything! But even if it was true, I couldn't change the fact that Alisa had just crashed horribly. That she was very sick and maybe dying. And that I couldn't do anything to help her.

As we walked down the corridor tears flowed down Mary K.'s face, a silent, steady stream.

There was nothing I could do to stop them.

15.
Lift

October 8, 1971

I'm so weak, I can hardly write this. I've told Mom and Dad that I have a bug so they won't bother me, but that's a lie. I've been in bed for over twenty-four hours. I can hardly sit up. And I can't stop crying.

I had to do it. Sam is still in the hospital, and I'm the one who put him there. Who would be next? My mother? My father? Me?

So last night I pulled the Harris Stoughton book from the shelf. It took only a moment to find the spell I was looking for—the same one I'd discovered accidentally the other day. The spell to strip one's self of magick.

I crept up to my room and prepared everything, the black candle, the cauldron. At first I was afraid that I wouldn't be able to pronounce the chants correctly—they were written in a language I didn't know. But as I started speaking, I found that the words flew off my tongue. For a moment I thought that the ceremony wouldn't be so bad.

I was wrong.

After a few minutes I began to feel like there was a weight on my tongue. Something slimy. As I continued the chants, the weight slipped down my throat, into the pit of my stomach, as if I'd swallowed a snake. It stayed there and started to grow. I kept chanting, but the weight grew and grew, choking me. It spread farther, down my arms, down my legs, until I felt like my entire body was filled with a giant, black serpent. I was gagging on it, gasping for air. The weight pressed me against the floor, crushing me. I thought my spine would crack, but it didn't, and soon the weight turned into a searing pain. Then, thankfully, the whole room went black.

I woke up on the floor of my room, feeling like a tree that's been hit by lightning. Alive on the outside but dead on the inside . . . rotting away. I'll never use my magick again. I hardly even know what I am.

And I still have the book. I've hidden it under my mattress until I can decide what to do with it. I can't bring myself to destroy it, and I can't let it fall into the wrong hands.

I can't think about this now. All I want to do is sleep. Forever.

    —Sarah Curtis

I was just about to crawl into bed when I heard the call. *Morgan.* The instant the word sounded in my mind, I knew that it was Hunter. He was sending me a witch message. I reached for the lapis lazuli by my bed. Lying back, I focused my energies and placed the smooth stone on my forehead. At the next heartbeat I felt Hunter, as if he were within me.

We have Ciaran.

For a moment they were words without meaning. I had spent the last several hours worrying about Alisa, terrified that I'd somehow hurt her, so it took me a moment to remember that there were other terrors in my life. Then images came into my mind, images of my birth father being bound by the braigh, of him crying out in pain, and I knew that Hunter was telling me that Ciaran had been apprehended by the council.

A thousand emotions rained down on me—relief, first, but then anger, and pity, and fear. And other feelings that I couldn't even identify. Ciaran's dark magick frightened and revolted me, but he was my *father*—the closest blood relative I had ever known. And when I remembered what I knew of witches who had had their power stripped—David Redstone, who had suffered horribly, or even how awful I'd felt when my power was only reined—I felt a horrible dread in the pit of my stomach. My father, my evil father. Captured. And utterly changed.

He will be stripped of his magick soon, Hunter's voice said in my mind. *First he must stand trial. But Morgan, apparently he had a few things in his possession that led the council to conclude that he definitely was targeting you for attacks.*

I frowned. *What things?*

Hunter was slow to respond. *The council won't release all of the information, but they said that he had a strand of your hair in a small box in his breast pocket.*

I sucked in my breath, wondering how Ciaran could have gotten a strand of my hair. But of course, it would have been easy. We spent plenty of time together. He could easily have found one of my hairs on his own jacket, for example.

They've also pulled in Lenore Ammett, Hunter went on. *According to her own Book of Shadows, she doesn't need proximity for telekinesis.*

My chest felt hollow. That was it, then. It was true. My own father had practically tried to kill me. Why? I wondered. What could he possibly gain by hurting me? *Morgan,* Hunter went on, *now that Ciaran is in custody, I think we should lift the deflection spell. There's no telling what might happen to him if he is stripped while still under the spell—and there's no need for it anymore, anyway. Erin is here, and she agrees with me.*

In a few moments I saw Erin's familiar face and twinkling eyes. She was sitting in a room surrounded by candles. Her face was lit with a golden glow. I felt the delicate bones of her hands in mine, and I knew that she and Hunter were holding hands. They were ready to begin the circle.

I had to blink back tears. Although I had feared that Ciaran might have been behind the strange accidents all along, somehow finding out for certain didn't fill me with relief; it filled me with sadness. I'd known he could be incredibly cruel, but a small part of me simply didn't want to believe that he was capable of hurting me. He was my birth father, after all. My only living parent. To know that he had actually tried to harm me, even knowing I was his daughter, was almost incomprehensible. And I couldn't understand why.

Can we have the circle without Sky and Alyce? I asked.

Sky has already left, Hunter replied, *and Alyce is busy with the store. But it doesn't require as much magick to release the spell as to put it in place. The three of us can do it.*

All right, I said. *But first I have to tell you something.* I took a deep breath. *Alisa is very sick. She's in the hospital. Mary K. and I went to see her this afternoon, and she had some kind of crash. I'm worried.* I didn't tell him that I might have been responsible for what had happened. I simply couldn't allow myself to think those thoughts.

That's terrible, Hunter replied. I could feel his concern, then confusion as he added, *Do you think we should send some healing spells her way?*

No, I don't think that's such a good idea. Even though I felt certain that I hadn't actually performed any magick that afternoon, that Alisa's crash was just a coincidence, the idea of doing a spell for her was terrifying. What if we ended up hurting her? I couldn't take the chance. *Alisa quit the coven,* I explained. *I don't know if she would want a spell done for her. And I wouldn't want to do anything against her wishes.*

All right, Hunter conceded, even though I could tell he wasn't entirely convinced. *Let me know how she's doing, won't you, Morgan?*

Of course, I promised. I inhaled deeply, bracing myself for the task to come. *Let's begin,* I said with Hunter's voice.

Erin began a low hum at the back of her throat, then, in a voice that was almost a whisper, she began to chant.

Let us now unwork the magick that encircles the blameworthy,
Leave him to his own strategy,
Just or fell.

The words went on, and the magick that welled up in me was like cool, clear water, fluid and bracing. I waited for Erin to pull out Harris Stoughton's book, and I was surprised to realize that she wasn't going to. She didn't even seem to have the book with her. Instead she reached for a large white dish and a white teapot. With a steady hand she filled the dish with steaming liquid. My nostrils were filled with the scent of mint and rosemary, and I nearly laughed to realize that my connection with Hunter was so strong that I could actually *smell* what he smelled. Reaching into a green velvet pouch beside her, Erin pulled out a handful of something and crumbled it into the water. The water shimmered for a moment, like the ocean in the setting sun. There was a light hissing sound and the scent of lavender, then Erin looked up and smiled.

"We have released the witch from his own restraints." Erin sounded as happy and relieved as I felt. "He will no longer be his own victim."

I inhaled deeply, still taking pleasure in the beautiful smells that lingered around me. Undoing the deflection spell had been as beautiful and easy as putting it on had been ugly and horrible. I felt wonderful now, even though the magick hadn't been directed at me. I was safe now—Ciaran couldn't threaten me any longer, and my magick was intact.

Morgan, thank you, Hunter's voice echoed in my mind.
For what?

There was a moment before he replied. *For everything,* he said finally. *For everything,* he repeated, soft as the sound of water flowing over smooth stones. In the next moment he was gone.

The lapis lazuli made a slight click as I placed it back on the nightstand and turned off the lamp. I love you, Hunter Niall, I thought as I pulled the comforter up to my chin. I looked out my window, into the depths of the starry sky.

"I did it." Bree leaned against a bank of lockers, clutching her books to her chest. There were dark circles under her eyes, as if she hadn't slept well.

"You talked to Robbie?"

Bree gave a faint nod.

"How did it go?" I asked. It was five minutes to the first bell.

"Badly," Bree said. "But better than I thought it would."

"So are you . . ." I didn't know how to finish the sentence.

"We're still together," Bree replied, tucking her silky hair behind one ear. "He was hurt, though. Really hurt about the stuff with Matt." She looked at me, her eyes rimmed with red. "That was the worst part. I've never—"

"I know," I said. "It's okay."

"He said that he loved me." Bree's voice was small and fragile, like a little girl's teacup. "I'm glad I told him, even though it wasn't easy."

We stood there a moment, not saying anything.

"I guess I'm afraid," Bree said finally.

I thought about Bree—about all the nights she ate dinner alone because her father was out of town on business. I thought about the brother she hadn't spoken to in over a month, the mother she hadn't seen in years. Bree knew about difficult love. No wonder she was afraid. "Robbie is special," I told her. "And you're strong."

Bree nodded, as if what I'd said was something she knew already—something she'd forgotten. She squeezed my hand, then let it go. "You're strong, too."

The bell rang, and we were swept down the hall toward homeroom in a churning sea of students. Neither one of us said anything more. Neither one of us had to.

16.
Letting Go

October 14, 1971

I couldn't hide it from them forever. Even though I tried.

My parents wanted to take me to see John Walter, the best healer in our coven. I knew he'd tell them the truth, so finally I had to admit what I'd done. My mother cried for two days, and my father stopped speaking to me altogether. My parents had always told me that there was nothing I could do that would make them stop loving me.

But I guess I found the one thing.

There's nothing I can do about it now. I couldn't bring my magick back even if I wanted to. And I don't want to. Even though I'm still weak from the ceremony, I would rather feel pain myself than run the risk of putting someone else in danger. I know that Wicca is dangerous. Beautiful, but dangerous. I just wish that someone would talk to me, would try to understand why I did what I did. Don't they understand that I've lost even more than they have?

I write this from a Greyhound bus bound for Houston. It was the farthest place from Gloucester for the smallest amount of money. Even so, it took most of my cash—I've only got twenty-three dollars and thirty-seven cents in my pocket . . . what's left of my life savings. With that, and a small bag of clothing, and the Harris Stoughton book wrapped in a black cloth (it's no danger to me any longer, and how could I leave such an evil book with my family?), I begin my new life.

I keep trying to tell myself that this kind of change is exactly what I need. That nothing has changed in my family for centuries and that I'm a pioneer, off to explore new worlds. I'm not really buying it, though.

It might be easier if I had some idea of where all of this would lead. But I don't.

I guess no one ever really does.

—Sarah Curtis

"Morgan?" Mary K.'s voice echoed up the stairway. I put my book aside and stood up. I had been lying on my bed, reading my English assignment, with Dagda curled comfortably in the curve of my waist.

Mary K. called up again, with more urgency this time. "Morgan!"

"What? What is it?" I stepped out of my room and

peered down the stairs. Mary K. was standing at the bottom with a huge grin. "What's going on?"

"There's somebody here that you might like to see."

"Who?" I started walking down the stairs. Hunter? I thought hopefully. But no, I would have sensed him coming. Who else could she be talking about?

When I got to the bottom of the stairs, Mary K. was alone in the foyer. Was she playing a trick on me? "Well, who—"

I broke off. Alisa was sitting on the couch in the living room, looking small and pale. Her hair was pulled back in a ponytail, emphasizing her gaunt, delicate face. She looked up at me nervously. "Hi, Morgan."

"Wow, Alisa." She looked like she was still weak, but she was *there*, sitting in my living room, talking to me. I walked over to the couch and perched beside her. "I'm so glad you're okay. How do you feel?"

Alisa shrugged. "Depends when you ask me, I guess." She pulled her hands into her lap, and I could see that she was holding the red-and-white teddy bear that Mary K. had brought to her hospital room. "I still feel weak, and I still have aches and dizziness every once in a while." She smiled a wan smile. "But I'm getting better. I'm well enough to leave my house, and that feels great."

Mary K. perched on my dad's armchair. "Do they know what made you sick?"

Alisa shook her head a little sadly. "Nobody seems to have any idea," she said. "After you two left, I got really bad, and the doctors were pretty worried. They told my father to start preparing for the worst. But after a few hours I just seemed to get better. And around midnight, I woke up really thirsty and asked the nurse for a glass of juice. I mean"—she gave a little laugh—"I'd been unconscious for, like, days, and I just up and asked for some apple juice out of the blue. The nurse was in shock."

"Wow." Mary K. looked at me as if to say, "Isn't that crazy?"

"I know," Alisa went on. "The doctors say it was a really bad virus and that the worst of it just had to pass through my system before I could start getting better." She looked at me meaningfully. "But the fact is, they don't really know what made me sick—and now they don't have any idea what made me better."

The way she was staring at me made me uncomfortable, and I looked away, out the window. Did she and Mary K. think that I'd cured her? But I hadn't. "Alisa, I—"

"Anyway," Alisa interrupted me, "I just wanted to say thank you. For coming to visit me in the hospital, I mean." She looked down into her lap and stroked the tiny red-and-white bear. Even though she was better, I still sensed a sadness in Alisa. I wondered about the family problems Mary K. had mentioned before.

"You're welcome," I said softly. I reached over to squeeze her arm. She seemed so down, and I still felt this weird protectiveness toward her. I wondered if I was starting to get maternal urges or something.

As I touched Alisa's arm, there was a crash. Alisa jumped. We all looked up to see that a framed photo had fallen off the mantel across the room. Frowning, Mary K. jumped up and picked it off the floor. "That's weird," she murmured, holding up a photo of our family around the tree last Christmas. "Must have been a draft."

I stared, frozen. There was no reason for that picture to fall off the mantel. No reason, that is, except the strange telekinetic incidents that had been following me. But that was Ciaran, I told myself. And Ciaran's in custody. He can't be doing this to me.

Was it possible that it was just a weird accident? Maybe I was making something out of nothing. If it had happened anytime before the past couple of weeks, I wouldn't have thought twice about it. It was just that so much had been happening lately . . . anything even vaguely out of the ordinary seemed suspicious.

Mary K. gingerly picked up the broken glass that surrounded the picture. As I watched her, I had a more frightening thought: What if it wasn't Ciaran who had been behind those incidents? What if it was someone else—someone else who was after me, and still on the loose?

"Um, I'd better get back to my homework," I blurted, standing up. "Alisa, I'm really glad you're feeling better. I hope I'll see you back at school soon."

"Thanks."

As I left the room, my eyes fell on the photo. Mary K. had propped it, still in the broken frame, on an end table while she picked up the glass. I shuddered when I saw how it had broken. Deep cracks had formed that set Mary K., my mom, and my dad in one section. In the other section was me, alone.

I sprinted back up to my room.

But before I even had time to think about what had happened, Mom knocked on my bedroom door. "Do you have a minute?" she called.

"Sure," I said as my mom opened the door and walked in, holding a sheaf of papers in her hand. I sighed. I could smell a lecture coming on. I knew what the papers were—it was the extra-credit assignment I'd written for Mr. Powell. He'd just handed it back that morning, with an A—that meant the full twenty points of extra credit. I'd been so excited about it that I'd left it out on the kitchen table for my mom to see, but now I remembered. She hadn't been so thrilled that I'd chosen to write about the persecution of witches. No doubt she wanted to tell me that this wouldn't be an appropriate application essay for Saint Anne's.

"Morgan," my mom said as she settled at the edge of my bed, "I like to think I'm a reasonable person."

Usually, I said mentally. But I didn't say anything out loud; I just nodded.

"That's why I—" But she couldn't finish. She just looked at the paper and shook her head.

"Look, I didn't mean to upset you," I said finally. "I just left it out because I thought you'd be glad that my grades are coming up."

"I know," my mom said slowly. "And you were right—I *am* glad." She flipped through the paper. "This is very well written, Morgan. You must have done a lot of research for it."

"A lot," I agreed. "But it's not hard when you're research-ing something you're really interested in."

My mom nodded and pursed her lips. "I always told you girls that I'd never stand in the way of things you were inter-ested in," she said. "At the time, I thought that was such an easy promise to make." She looked down at the paper again. "Morgan, I think your father and I made a mistake when we considered sending you to Catholic school."

For a moment I thought I'd misheard her or hallucinated or something.

"That was the wrong solution," my mom went on. "I guess we—or I guess I—just overreacted. "I . . ." My mom stopped to take a deep breath. "I hope you know that I'm just afraid for you, Morgan. I love you, that's all," she finished in a whisper.

I felt a wave of relief wash over me. She was serious—no Catholic school! Thank the Goddess! And with that wave of relief came a rush of love and gratitude for my mom, who was putting aside her fear and allowing me to explore something she didn't understand. I leaned over and took the paper from her hand. "Thank you so much," I said softly. "I know Wicca frightens you. But it's part of me, Mom. I can't change it."

My mother was silent for so long that I thought perhaps I'd upset her. But finally she said, "You're right." She sighed and shook her head. "Morgan, I'm your mother, and I want you to be happy. I was concerned when I saw your grades suffering. But now you've shown me that you're bringing them up. You've even proved that your interests and your academics can peacefully coexist." She looked at me. "I don't want to be the kind of mother who tells you what to believe. I swore to myself that I'd never be like that, and I intend to keep that promise. No matter how hard it is."

I leaned over and hugged her, breathing in the light, sweet smell of her perfume. It occurred to me how much I had missed her—how much I had missed my whole family— in the last few weeks. Now I was safe, Ciaran was in custody, and I had my family around me. I felt warm and happy. My mom kissed me on the forehead. "I think that this hard work deserves a little reward," she said. "What do you suggest?"

I lifted my eyebrows and grinned. "The end of my grounding period?"

"How about a phone call?"

"Good enough," I said quickly, scrambling out of bed. Dagda let out a mew of complaint.

"Where are you going?" my mom asked.

I turned and grinned at her. "To go call Hunter."

"Ah," she said with a smile. "Well, tell him I said hello."

"I will," I called over my shoulder as I practically ran down the stairs. I couldn't wait to tell him the good news about Alisa—I couldn't wait to tell him everything. I was in such a hurry as I punched in Hunter's number on the cordless phone that I messed up twice. I took a deep breath and tried again.

Hunter answered on the first ring. "Morgan, I'm so glad you called," he said.

I laughed for what seemed like the first time in weeks. I hadn't spoken to Hunter in days, and his voice seemed delicious to me. It was true that the mind melds we'd been having were great, but there was something so comforting about hearing his voice on the phone, so normal, that it almost made me giddy. "I guess there's no point in trying to surprise you with a phone call," I said lightly. "Guess what! No Catholic school!"

There was a moment of quiet on the other end of the line. For a second I wondered whether he'd heard me. "Morgan, love, that's brilliant. Is it because you've brought your grades up?"

"It is," I said happily. "Oh, and Alisa's okay! She stopped by earlier."

"Oh, excellent."

I paused, thinking about Alisa's visit and the picture falling. Should I tell Hunter about that? Or would he just think I was paranoid?

"Morgan—" Hunter began. There was something in his tone. What was it? Concern? Fear?

"What is it?" A feeling of dread spread through the pit of my stomach.

"I've heard from Sky."

It took a moment for the news to sink in. "What did she—"

"She's found some leads," Hunter went on. "In fact, she believes my parents are not in France."

"No?" I felt a sudden, horribly selfish wave of relief. Did that mean Hunter wouldn't have to go to Europe to search for them?

"No," Hunter replied. "She believes they're in Canada. Quebec. It would explain the French. I'm going to head up there myself, as soon as possible."

The room started to tilt crazily, and I had to hold on to the counter for support. "But—but—the council—"

"I've spoken with the council," Hunter said. "Morgan, Ciaran is in custody. Selene and Cal are gone." He paused. "I've asked permission to investigate the Canada leads. There's no reason for me to be here now." He sighed. "Don't you see? You're safe now. There isn't anything left for me to do in Widow's Vale."

Had he really just said that? "Thanks a lot," I said bitterly, swallowing the tears that were welling up in my throat.

"That isn't what I meant, and you know it," Hunter said quietly.

I did know. But it hurt anyway. "How long will you be gone?" I asked.

"It's hard to be sure," Hunter replied. "It could be a few days or a few weeks. Or longer. It depends on what I find."

Of course. That was what I was afraid of. The image I'd seen when I scried, the image of Hunter waving farewell, entered my mind, along with the feeling of dread I'd felt when I first saw it. Was it possible . . . was it possible that he might *never* come back? Don't think that way, I commanded myself, but it was too late. I thought of the picture falling earlier, how frightened I had been. Had something so small really seemed so important just a few minutes ago?

"Just how reliable is Sky's information?" I demanded. The moment the words were out of my mouth, I hated myself for saying them. But I couldn't stop. "What if you're heading into some kind of trap?"

Hunter didn't reply. He didn't have to. We both knew that Sky would never have told Hunter he should go to Canada unless she had some overwhelming evidence.

I pulled out a chair and sat down at the breakfast table, my forehead in my palm. This can't be happening, I thought dizzily. Now that I was safe, Hunter was leaving. I tried to focus on my breathing, on pulling the fresh air into my lungs and letting the old air go. For a crazy moment I wished that I could be in some sort of horrible danger. It was a very strange thing, to realize that I would rather have my life in jeopardy with Hunter than to be safe . . . without him.

"Morgan," Hunter said. His voice grew quieter. "We're mùirn beatha dàns. You know I love you completely. But you also know how I feel about my parents. You wouldn't want me to pass up this chance, would you?"

Yes, I thought. I opened my mouth to say it, but I couldn't. How could I tell him that? What would it do to our love?

"No," I whispered. "I want you to find them."

"I knew that was what you would say." Hunter's voice was a caress.

I inhaled. I exhaled. I ran my fingers over the ridges of the cotton place mat. It felt impossibly normal to me, incongruously simple.

Out of nowhere, the words Alisa had spoken over a week ago echoed in my mind. *I wish things could stay the way they are.* For a brief moment I'd been safe, my family had been happy, and I'd known who my mùirn beatha dàn truly was. And now he was leaving me. I remembered the vision I'd had, the one in which Hunter had waved good-bye, and I tried not to think that this separation was permanent.

Trust me. The words hadn't been spoken, yet they seemed to be all around me, spinning lazily like dandelion fluff on a summer wind. I looked out the kitchen window. The night was dark, and the moon was out. I couldn't see any stars, but I knew they were there. I could picture them, waiting patiently, their light cutting through the infinite darkness. Fire had never looked so cold to me.

Trust me.

What choice did I have?

"I do," I said.